Forbidden Climb

Gavin Baird

AuthorGavinBaird.com

Contents

Chapter 1

After a long shift, Ethan's nose had become accustomed to the smell of ozone and burnt metal, so the brisk, evening air shocked his lungs like a splash of chilly water. Taking another deep breath, he strolled through the parking lot towards his truck.

It was Friday night going into a long weekend, so he didn't need to return to the welding shop until Tuesday. While he didn't have any specific plans for the weekend, he and his friends often planned things the day that they happened, and he was sure that would hold true tomorrow.

His drive home took him through the wide suburbs of Corvallis. Near the end of the trip, Ethan passed a vacant house. The house hadn't been vacant for long, less than a month, in fact, but the evidence of vacancy was visible. Unlike the other houses on the street, it was completely dark; no lamps lit the windows, and no television screen danced in the living room. Ethan used to know the man that lived there. He wouldn't have considered him a friend; they were just acquaintances.

Like Ethan, the man was in his early twenties, fit and healthy, and he enjoyed the outdoors: backpacking, hiking, mountain biking, and other outdoor sports. That love for nature got him killed.

That was the theory, anyway. In the past six months, scores of other outdoors men and women had disappeared without a trace, all of them going missing in the Siuslaw National Forest, among the lush slopes of the Oregon Coast Range, beneath the ancient and stoic Douglas Firs.

The Forest Service said that they were all killed by mountain lions, and that the bodies were unrecoverable, but something about that didn't sit right with Ethan. Sure, once in a blue moon a cougar would be spotted in the McDonald Research forest, which was less than a mile away from Ethan's home, but they never attacked anyone. Especially not in the numbers that the Forest Service reported in the last month alone.

The roaring road noise created by the tires on Ethan's truck went quiet as he pulled into his driveway, and, turning the key, the engine shut off. The soles of his steel-toed boots scraped against the concrete path, then Ethan climbed the steps up to his porch.

Inside the house, he flicked on the porchlight so that his roommate, Alex, could find his way to the door when he came home from his night classes in a few hours.

Frowning, Ethan climbed the stairs to his room, pushed open the creaky door, and sat down on his bed. He stripped out of his dirty work clothes and put on a black cotton t shirt and a pair of basketball shorts, then he collapsed into his chair, reaching for his computer. The monitor flashed to life and Ethan typed in his password, ready to get lost in the expanse of the internet for the night. He browsed for a few hours and found himself gravitating towards forums and articles about cryptids and wilderness horror stories.

Long after the sun had set, the sound of the heavy front door opening echoed through the house. Alex's footsteps padded through the downstairs hallway, and Ethan heard him flick on the kitchen light. Ethan found a good stopping point in the story he was reading and put his computer to sleep.

Downstairs, Alex had claimed the entire dining room table with a spread of papers and dull-looking documents.

"I see you have a little bit of homework tonight," Ethan commented.

Letting out a dry laugh, Alex responded, "it's not homework actually."

"So, what is it?" Ethan asked, leaning towards the papers with renewed interest.

"I got these from a friend in the college of forestry. They collect extensive data on the populations of most animals that live in the forests around the state and, well, look here," he pointed at a column labelled *Puma Concolor*. "The mountain lion population is certainly healthy, but," he snatched another document, the paper crinkling in his grasp, "the population has already been slowly rising ever since 1994."

"So what?"

"Well, the Forest Service is saying that this year's spike in disappearances is caused by cougars, but their population is climbing at the same rate it has been for a decade. I guess it's possible that there are other factors driving them to attack people, but I find that unlikely, given that they prefer to avoid humans. I think that the disappearances are being caused by something else."

Primed by the horror stories he was just reading, Ethan's imagination whipped up a few outlandish possibilities. Most were ridiculous, like aliens or bigfoot. But Alex wasn't joking. In fact, based on the frown on his face, he was serious. Alex wasn't one to draw outlandish conclusions or make unfounded claims. If he was bringing this to Ethan, he meant business.

So, Ethan took him seriously, and his train of thought moved away from cryptids to real possibilities. The Forest Service said that the disappearances were caused by cougars. Nothing obvious was causing the cougars to attack more people. Therefore, the Forest Service was lying.

The room fell silent and a sinister mood permeated the air. Ethan crossed his arms and looked down. He paused for a few tense moments then announced, "It's a coverup, then."

Ethan thought about his group of backpacking friends—which included Alex—and concluded that they would want to know about this. They all knew how to deal with a mountain lion, any capable outdoorsman does. That is why Ethan wasn't worried at first when the disappearances started happening. They were easy to dismiss as inexperienced hikers who stumbled into a cougar and panicked. But now, he didn't know what the threat even was.

"We need to talk to the guys about this," he said, pacing around the cluttered table, "maybe they will have some ideas for what to do."

"Well, Eric is already coming over tomorrow to hang out with me, let's call Mike and Todd to see if they can too."

Ethan nodded, "we need to organize another backpacking trip soon, anyway."

Alex continued to study the documents, occasionally reaching for a new one every few moments, causing the whole table to rustle with the sound of moving paper. Ethan stayed for a while, but whatever Alex was looking for was above Ethan's paygrade, so he went back upstairs to get ready for bed.

As he lay there, his initial fear and suspicion regarding the disappearances morphed into curiosity. Of course, the unknown danger scared him a bit, but it was different than worrying about cougars. He was used to planning to deal with animals, it was part of backpacking, but they were more annoying than anything. A coverup, however? That was exciting. Ethan drifted to sleep despite his overactive imagination.

Chapter 2

Mike, Todd, and Eric brought their packs to Ethan's house on Saturday morning. Last night, Ethan didn't say much on the phone to them, just that there was something important they needed to talk about regarding their backpacking trips. Of course, they assumed that they were planning a regular expedition—and they weren't completely wrong—but the trip that Ethan had in mind was nothing but regular.

Sitting around the cluttered dining room table, Ethan and Alex explained how they discovered the discrepancy regarding the disappearances, and the three other men came to the same conclusion that something was being covered up.

Mike frowned, tapping his fingers against the table, "so, what are we going to do about it?" he asked, "you can't seriously be suggesting that we avoid the forest just because you're afraid of some enigma."

Ethan ignored the insult and responded, "no, I'm not saying that we avoid the forest, I'm suggesting the opposite. We should hike in and see if we can find anything. Eric and I don't have work on Monday and the rest of you don't have classes, which gives us three days to explore if we go today."

"But where?" asked Todd, "the forest is massive, we couldn't cover the whole thing in a lifetime."

Alex grabbed a thin packet and slid it towards Todd. "You remember when our neighbor went missing?" He gestured at the papers, "this article says that they found his car, and the news reported on it before they could hide the location. It's the only story I could find where the exact location of the disappearance is noted."

Eric said, "you know, I'm down to go on a trip today, but why do we have to go searching now? Why don't we just go on a shorter trip near Jawbone Flats or something?"

Ethan shrugged, "I guess we don't really have to go today, but something about this is bothering me, and the longer we wait, more people could get hurt by whatever they are covering up."

Mike scoffed at that, "because that's our job? We aren't detectives and we aren't with search and rescue. For all we know, nosy backpackers like us could be causing the problem."

"You don't have to come with me if you don't want to," Ethan said with an even tone. "It is possible that there isn't anything we can do, but I have to see for myself." *And I don't know if I could bear the curiosity much longer,* he thought to himself.

"Count me in," Eric said, putting a hand on his pack, "let's dive into this rabbit hole. If nothing else, it'll make for an interesting backpacking trip, and we've been through worse. Remember when we had to hide in that cave? In the burn out by Jefferson?" He chuckled, then broke into a full laugh that the rest of the group joined in on.

Once the laughter faded, Ethan looked at Alex. He assumed that Alex was on board, but he hadn't asked him yet. Alex's nod confirmed his assumption. Todd agreed to go as well, and Mike's stubborn expression softened as he acquiesced, saying, "alright, I won't say no to a good hike."

From under the table, Alex pulled out an atlas. He opened it to a page that was marked with a sticky note as a bookmark. Near the center of the page was the most notable feature: Mary's Peak. And a little bit over was a hand-drawn circle on an unmarked road in the middle of the wilderness. Pointing at it, Alex said, "this is where our neighbor's car went missing. It's the best spot to start our search."

Studying the map of the area, Ethan rubbed his chin. The stubble on his face reminded him that he still hadn't shaved today. "I'm guessing that we'll have to walk thirty miles in total, which, for experienced hikers like us, should be a three-day expedition."

"Sounds good," Alex said. Looking around the room, he said, "I'm assuming that everyone has all of their gear, minus food?"

His assumption was confirmed by nods from everyone.

"Good, I have enough trail food for everybody in the pantry here."

They busied themselves preparing their packs. Alex portioned enough food and distributed it among the guys, who diligently stuffed it into their packs. They walked out the front door, carrying their gear. Ethan imagined that they looked very rugged from a distance, with their expensive equipment.

To Ethan only, Alex said, "this whole situation is making me nervous. Something suspicious is going on. I trust you to keep us safe and make the right decisions out there, but be extra watchful."

Ethan knew that Alex was much smarter than himself. He was more logical too. So, the fact that Alex was trusting his gut meant something was up. It made Ethan anxious. That anxiety was drastically outweighed by Ethan's reckless curiosity, however.

After final checks and one last review of the plan, Ethan loaded all five packs into the back of his truck, then slammed shut the tailgate and the canopy window. The engine roared to life: his truck was eager to get out of the suburbs and onto some rougher terrain.

Sitting shotgun next to Ethan, Alex asked, "what do you think is really doing it?"

"Doing what? Causing the disappearances?" He chuckled, "I have no idea, but I was thinking about it. Obviously, the statistics told us that the cougars weren't to blame, but I don't think that any other predator is either."

"How so?"

"All of the hikers disappeared without a trace. I've read everything I can find about what's been going on in that forest," he gestured forward to the West, at the looming mountains, "and in every case, they vanish without so much as a pine needle out of place. If something is hunting people, there would be evidence of a death struggle, or some remains left behind that the scavengers didn't want, but there is literally nothing. Not even a torn piece of clothing, nothing."

"So, aliens?"

Ethan let out a dry laugh, "I haven't seen any flashing lights in the sky, have you?"

The highway was packed with other drivers travelling to the coast to spend their weekends on the beach. Then Ethan left the highway for the rough forest roads. Breaking away from the westbound routes, he saw only a handful of other cars. Moss drooped from the craggy tree branches, and not much light filtered to the ground, blocked by the canopy above. The tires of Ethan's truck crunched against the untraveled gravel roads.

About ten miles West of Mary's Peak, Ethan parked his truck in a patch of grass on the side of the road. It took him a few moments, but he spotted a sign affixed to a rotting post on the opposite side of the forest road. He couldn't read the faded lettering, but he assumed that it was a trailhead.

"This place looks like it hasn't been visited in a decade," Eric scoffed. "I guess that makes it a great spot to go missing." He poked the trailhead marker with a trekking pole, causing it to topple over onto a fern.

Ethan walked around to the back of his truck and unlocked the tailgate, then he unloaded everyone's packs. He shouldered his own and buckled the hip straps, securing the familiar weight. Once the other guys finished prepping their gear, Ethan locked up his truck and stuffed the key into his pants pocket. He took a deep breath of the forest air, drinking in the smell of the fir trees. Despite the shade from the towering, ancient trees, the wilderness felt lively and animated; needles and leaves rustled in the wind, and small birds flitted through the canopy many stories above. He could have easily forgotten the ominous circumstances of their trip.

"They probably don't want it to look like it's been visited," Ethan said.

"Do you think there are guards?" Alex asked.

"I swear, Ethan, I'm going to be so pissed if you just led us into a restricted area," Mike said.

"Oh, quit being so paranoid," Ethan said.

Eric led the way up the trail, with Ethan taking the rear. The five men were forced to hike in a single-file line to stay on the thin trail. Ferns and crabgrass reached from either side of the already rough dirt path, leaving only a thin patch of dirt visible in the middle.

Aside from the condition of the trail, hiking through the forest put little strain on the men. With the shade of the trees protecting them from sunburns, the temperature was exactly right; breaking a light sweat would be the worst of their exertion. It was like the forest was pulling them deeper and deeper into its protection.

After about forty yards of walking, Ethan turned around to take one last look at his truck, and noticed a second, white truck pulling up next to the trailhead. Looking over his shoulder, Ethan watched the truck for a few moments, but it had no visible markings, and the license plates indicated that it was a private vehicle, so he assumed that it was simply another group of hikers, and he neglected to tell his friends about the new truck.

The sun continued its arc across the sky, and Ethan's group continued deeper into the wilderness. Small animals like snakes and squirrels darted through the forest around them, but there were still no signs of large predators, although, Ethan realized, any cougars would likely avoid them until nighttime.

A few hours after they started hiking, they stopped for lunch. Ethan and his friends sat on the edge of a thin, silent creek, snacking on granola bars and beef jerky. There was still no sign of other hikers, and Ethan found himself looking back the trail every few minutes. He hated to stay in one spot. Hastily crunching on his trail food, Ethan felt like he was being watched.

"We're losing daylight, guys, let's get as far as we can and then we can pick a spot to rest for the night."

"Come on, Ethan, just let us have a break. I'm really getting into this jerky," Eric said.

"No, you can eat your jerky while we walk. Let's go."

Splashing through the creek, Ethan took the lead. "Slow down, Ethan!" Alex shouted at him. Alex trotted closer to Ethan. Once he was right behind, he said in a quieter tone, "why are you going so fast, did you see something?"

Biting the inside of his cheek, Ethan frowned and said, "there was another truck that parked right next to mine right when we started hiking. I thought they might have been other hikers, but I still haven't seen anyone else yet. It's making me nervous, that's all."

Reflexively looking over his shoulder, Alex asked, "should we tell the others?"

"I don't think so, it wouldn't do them any good, but we should keep our guard up."

"It was probably just another group of guys that had the same idea as we did," Alex muttered dismissively.

The sun was low in the sky when they decided to make camp. It was in the perfect spot: a handful of paces off the trail and in a clearing with a few young maple trees. Ethan and Mike strung up their hammocks and tarps while the rest of the guys staked down their lightweight tents. Rays of orange light beamed through the camp, the products of the low-hanging sun and the numerous fir trees that stood as tall and straight as telephone poles.

In the evening light, the men boiled water with their Jetboils and used it to prepare freeze-dried meals. Mike, Todd, and Eric talked and gestured vividly about something Ethan didn't care to pay attention to; both he and Alex spent their mealtime watching the edges of their camp and the trail with narrowed eyes.

Once the last dregs of sunlight faded from the sky, all that lit the camp were a few scattered patches of moonlight. The conversation faded and the men sluggishly prepared to go to sleep. Ethan was the last one to go. For a while, he sat in the quiet forest and continued to scan his surroundings. Eventually, his eyelids grew heavy and he slid into his hammock's warm embrace, nodding off to the sound of leaves swaying in the wind.

Chapter 3

Ethan gasped and sat up in his hammock. He looked at his watched, only to discover that he went to sleep just a couple of hours ago. Taking a few deep breaths to calm himself, he shakily relaxed back into his hammock.

Closing his eyes, Ethan listened to the sounds of the forest. The wind was much louder now, and it had a strange tone to it. The wind didn't wax and wane as a normal breeze would, no, it was a static whooshing noise. It sounded less like wind and more like a distant leaf blower.

Ethan was unsure if he was hearing correctly, assuming that he was still partly asleep. He was used to having strange dreams.

But something else was missing too. Ethan leaned over the edge of his hammock and looked out from under his tarp at one of the maple trees around his camp. Despite the high winds, the tree's leaves didn't move an inch. Looking back at his own tarp, Ethan realized that it too was unaffected by the wind.

Ethan extended an arm out from his sleeping bag and held it up to the air. It was calm. No wind at all. "What the hell," Ethan muttered under his breath.

He sat awkwardly in his hammock with his torso propped up by one arm. Upon further observation, Ethan discovered that the noise was coming from every direction around him, and it had no depth at all. For all he knew, it could be coming from twenty feet away, or twenty miles.

Mike seemed unaffected by the noise. He was fast asleep in his own hammock just a few feet to Ethan's right. Ethan considered waking his friend but decided to wait and listen to the odd sound for a few more moments.

Soon, the constant whooshing was joined by a faint, pulsing rasp that Ethan could not make out. The rasp pulsed faster. Its rate increased for a few seconds until the rasp stopped altogether.

From every direction, the noise grew louder, then the rasp returned. It sounded like a sick person's shaky breathing. Then Ethan's eyes grew wide. *The noise! It's whispering!*

"E-Ethan!" the forest rasped and stuttered. Then the wind stopped, and the voices didn't return.

He froze like a deer in the headlights, searching around camp for whatever called his name. Adrenaline coursed through his veins. He tried to make sense of what just happened, but in his sleep deprived state, thinking clearly was impossible.

Ethan let out a quick bark of laughter. "Am I going insane?" he whispered to himself before collapsing back into his hammock. It didn't take long for his exhaustion from yesterday's hike to overcome his shock, and Ethan quickly fell back asleep.

Chapter 4

"I think this conspiracy theory is making you paranoid, Ethan," Eric said over a bowl of instant oatmeal. He dipped his spork into his bowl, took another bite, and with a mouth full of food, added, "that was probably just sleep paralysis or some really vivid nightmare."

Ethan sipped from his cup of tea and retorted, "well it couldn't have been sleep paralysis because I was able to move. And the sound was so loud! You're seriously saying that none of you heard it?"

"Seriously, we didn't," Mike said.

Ethan scowled down at his tea, retreating to his hammock to start breaking camp. Within a few moments, Alex approached him and muttered, "I heard the noise too, I just didn't want to tell the group."

Through narrowed eyes, Ethan studied Alex then asked, "what did it sound like to you?"

"Just a bunch of whispering that I couldn't understand. I thought it was a part of my dream and I just went back to sleep. I never left my tent."

"Something in this forest is not right. There is some weird shit out here and we're getting close to it. Maybe there's a good reason that the Forest Service is covering it up."

"So, we're back to aliens again?" Alex chuckled.

With a smirk, Ethan replied, "come on, let's get packed up, we have a lot of walking to do today."

The rest of the day went by uneventfully, and there was still no sign of other hikers in the area. While hiking, Ethan scanned the forest, looking for anything that could explain the whispering. He didn't see anything.

In the evening, the wind picked up. It howled through the forest much louder than yesterday, and again, the forest was unaffected by the gust.

"Do you guys hear that?" Alex shouted.

"Of course, I hear the wind, what about it?" Eric demanded.

In response, Alex simply pointed that the unmoving tree branches above. This time, however, the noise had a point of origin. "Alex, listen!" Ethan said, hushing the chatter coming from the others. He pointed forward up the trail and slightly to the right, "it's coming from that direction!"

"Do you want to go there?" Alex shouted over the din.

"Do we have any other choice? That's where the trail goes, and I really want to find out what's making the noise."

For half an hour they advanced along the trail, following the noise. As they got closer, it got louder, and soon enough, the pulsing rasp—that Ethan knew to be whispering—started.

Wincing, Eric asked in disbelief, "is that," he paused, "whispering?"

Slowly, as time passed and they got closer to the place it was coming from, the rasp became clearer. It became obvious that it was trying to say something. Strangely, the volume was quite paradoxical. The noise was deafening, and the raspy voices tore at Ethan's ears, but it gave the perception of near silence. Hence, Ethan couldn't make out what the voices were saying.

"I can't understand what it's saying. It sounds like hundreds of whispering voices talking all at once. They're saying something, but I can't tell what," Alex said.

Ethan strained to interpret the cryptic whispering, but whenever he thought that he recognized a word or phrase it was drowned out by ten other voices. It called, "here… below… almost time… but… eat," and continued to get louder.

Soon, the noise came from a direction perpendicular and to the right of the trail. "It's this way, guys, we have to leave the trail," Ethan commanded.

Mike grumbled something about getting lost, but Ethan ignored him; he had to know what was making the noise. Instead, Ethan pulled a compass from his pocket. The noise was coming from the west. *Okay, we need to go east to get back to the trail*, he thought to himself before trampling through the underbrush of the forest floor. At this point, the whispering was louder than his own breathing. Ethan slashed his way through the forest for a few hundred feet, until he eventually breached a clearing.

In the center was a staircase. Ethan blinked and rubbed his eyes.

The clearing was at least ninety feet wide, and the ground was covered in tall grass. All the trees around the edge of the clearing leaned away from the staircase in the center, as if they were afraid of it. As for the staircase itself, it was the same kind of staircase that would be seen in someone's house. It rose to about fifteen feet in the air and was supported by cream-white drywall around its base. Ethan guessed that there had to be some framing underneath, but none was visible. Its steps were carpeted like a regular domestic staircase. The stairs showed no sign of weathering, either, and there was nothing at the top—they led to empty air. Without a doubt, the whispering was coming from the stairs. Ethan looked back at his friends to see that they were just as confused as he was.

Ethan gingerly stepped towards the bizarre structure. The grass around its base was brown and dying. Mike and

Todd stayed back from the stairs while Ethan, Alex, and Eric circled the structure, looking for details—like plaques, signs, or any markings—that could allude to the purpose of the stairs. They found nothing.

The stairs radiated an evil energy that made Ethan shiver, and in that moment, Ethan realized that they must have something to do with the disappearances. He just wasn't sure what they did. Of course, a fall from the top wouldn't be enough to kill a healthy person, so it wasn't like they were a regular safety hazard.

"It's like somebody teleported them from inside a house to here," Alex said with a hand on the top of his head.

"Should we climb them?" Eric asked, kneeling at the base of the first step. He poked the carpet.

"Get the hell away from those!" a voice roared from behind them.

Ethan whipped around to see a Forest Ranger stomping towards them. The ranger grabbed Ethan by the neck, pulling him away from the stairs. Ethan stumbled to keep up with the ranger's iron grip. "Who are you? Get off me!" he yelled. The ranger threw him to the ground.

Laying in the dirt, Ethan squinted at the man and blurted, "was that you in the truck at the trailhead?"

The ranger ignored him, turning to his friends and shouting, "you four! Get over here!"

Getting up, Ethan demanded, "why can't we go up the stairs? What are they?"

Scowling at Ethan, the ranger stalked over to him and stared into his eyes. Their faces were just a few inches apart. "You stay away from those stairs, or I will put you down myself. Do not climb them. Do not go near them. Do not look at them. And ignore anything you hear them say."

"You didn't answer my questions!" Ethan spat, but the ranger was already turning away.

To the whole group, the ranger announced, "you're leaving right now. Start hiking back to your truck. If you need to stop and sleep the night, fine, but don't you dare turn back."

No one moved. Ethan scowled and remained steadfast. Who was this Forest Ranger to tell him what to do? He could be here on public land! Then the ranger reached for his belt, and Ethan noticed for the first time that a handgun was hanging there. The scowl fell from Ethan's face, and he felt a pump of adrenaline run through his body. The only weapon he had was a hunting knife, and it was stuffed in his backpack. There was no winning this fight.

They reluctantly left the clearing at the order of the ranger, but at the edge of the clearing Ethan stopped and asked the ranger, "are the stairs causing the disappearances?"

The ranger's face turned red with rage, but he didn't answer, simply pointing in the direction of the trail. Ethan clenched a fist behind his back, glanced back at the stairs and thought about his missing neighbor. He tensed up and almost threw a punch, but acquiesced at the last moment, following the direction of the ranger's gaze. *I will come back here*, he resolved.

Those stairs had to be it. That's what the Forest Service was covering up. Ethan tried to fathom how the ranger knew when they parked, and how he managed to track them for miles unnoticed. The amount of resources alone that they must be spending on keeping these stairs a secret… Ethan shook his head.

It made him angry. Their job was to maintain the forest for the community, and here they were forcing Ethan to leave. It wasn't like he was trespassing; the stairs were unmarked. Besides, he wouldn't have been so mad if the ranger explained to him what the stairs were, or how they were harmful. But instead, the service was covering them up.

That night, they made camp after hiking back for an hour. There was little conversation. The ranger sat on the edge of camp watching Ethan and his friends, ensuring that they wouldn't try to return to the stairs overnight.

Ethan noticed the ranger was starting to nod off, so he slid out of his hammock and padded over to Alex's tent. Still awake, Alex unzipped the door the second that Ethan whispered to announce his presence.

"Ethan, what is it?" he demanded in a groggy but quiet voice.

"Do you still have your gps with you?" he pointed at Alex's backpack.

"Yeah, I think so, but it's been off the whole trip."

"That's fine, we still aren't too far from the stairs."

"So what? We know where to park to get to the stairs."

"Just trust me," Ethan hushed him, taking the gps from Alex's outstretched hand. "How do you turn this thing on?"

Alex reached over and held a button on the top of the device. It looked like one of the old cell phones—the thick blocky ones that were the first to have touch screens—but inside of the device was the newest satellite communication technology. The screen flashed to life, and Ethan took a reading of their exact coordinates, then he wrote it down on a scrap of paper.

Ethan turned off the gps and handed it back to Alex, "thanks, that all I need," then returned to his hammock.

Chapter 5

The next day went by quickly. The ranger woke them up early and forced them to break camp and get moving. Instead of hiking at a relaxed pace, they went nearly twice as fast as they did when coming into the forest. By the time that they reached the parking lot, Ethan was panting and out of water.

Before Ethan drove off, the ranger approached his window and growled, "I better not see you near those ever again."

Ethan sneered and rolled up his window, and as soon as he pulled away, the cab of his truck exploded with conversation.

"It's ghosts," Eric yelled, "we just disturbed some sort of burial ground or holy sight. We're dead." He punched the headrest in front of him for added effect, causing Alex to turn around in annoyance.

"No, there has to be a rational explanation for it," Mike said.

Alex scoffed, "I wouldn't be so sure about that."

"Oh really? Why not? What is it then?"

"How should I know?" Alex asked, gesturing wildly, "but there is no normal explanation for those stairs. Even just the whispering! There would have to be some extremely powerful speakers for the sounds to be heard as far away as we were, and even if, and that's a big if, someone managed to get a concert-level sound system out there, there is absolutely no way they could get enough power to run it."

"Fine then," Mike shouted, "the stairs are paranormal! So what? It's not my problem, and it seems like the Forest Service has it under control."

"They don't have it under control at all!" Ethan interjected, "people are still going missing and they still haven't done anything about it!"

"How do you know that those stairs are causing the disappearances though? They didn't hurt us; all they did was whisper at us!"

Ethan said, "I am absolutely sure that they are the problem."

"Okay," Mike laughed, "well, what are you going to do about it?

"I'm going to go back."

"Ha! Count me out of that mission!"

"Same here, I don't want anything to do with this witch hunt," Todd said.

"I'm with you, Ethan," Eric affirmed, "I want to find out what the whispering was saying."

"Are you in, Alex?" Ethan asked.

"Yeah, I'm curious too."

"How are you guys going to get back to the stairs, I think it's obvious that they're watching the trailhead," Mike asked.

"We don't need the trailhead anymore," Ethan said, pulling the paper with the coordinates he recorded out of his pocket. "Someone, maybe you or Todd, could drop us off on a road, and we'll figure it out from there. We'll make our own trail. I know you don't want to go to the stairs, but it would mean a lot if you dropped us off."

"Yeah, sure, but I'm not going near those stairs again."

Ethan turned his attention back to the road ahead of him. The sun was setting. He was glad to be able to sleep in his own bed tonight. By the time that the stars became visible, Ethan had dropped off his friends, and he and Alex arrived home.

They unpacked their gear in the living room in silence—except for the sound of rustling fabric. Ethan looked at his scrap of paper that held the coordinates, grunted, and set it aside.

"What is it?" Alex asked, looking up from his gear.

"We were right," Ethan stated.

"About what?"

"They were covering something up."

"That's obvious," Alex laughed dryly, "but we still don't know what 'something' is."

"Alex, you're less superstitious than I am. I mean, you're a microbiology student, so of course you are but… what do you think those stairs are?"

Alex hesitated, staring down at the floor. "Whatever they are, they're evil."

Chapter 6

Ever since he got lost when he was a kid, Ethan practiced orienteering and navigation as if his life depended on it—and it did. He was ten years old when it happened. On a backpacking trip with his family, Ethan wandered off the trail when his parents weren't looking, and he couldn't find his way back. He was lost for hours. In the evening, however, he wandered onto a different trail and encountered a man and a woman that were hiking. They had a map of the area, and Ethan managed to give them the name of the lake that his family was at. Using his map and compass, the man guided Ethan back to his family, reuniting them. The skills that he learned over the years after that incident gave him confidence in his ability to make his way to the stairs without a trail.

Mike's car hummed to life. It had been a week since the first encounter with the stairs. The drive towards them was mostly the same as the first one, but at the end, Mike turned down a different dirt road, and instead of stopping at a parking lot, he pulled over to the side of the road, his car still idling. Ethan, Alex, and Eric took their backpacks from Mike's trunk.

They stood on the unpaved dirt road, barely wide enough for two cars to pass each other. A thin ditch ran on either side of it, but no runoff was there. Other than the road, they were in the middle of the wilderness. Ethan looked down the road and noticed a spot where the road jutted out to the side, creating what looked like a driveway. Of course, it didn't lead to anything, and it was only about ten yards long, but it would make the perfect spot to discreetly park a car. With some brush, Ethan thought, he could conceal it well enough that he wouldn't be worried about his truck being spotted by a forest ranger on patrol.

"I'll send you a message with the gps when we are ready to get picked up," Ethan said.

Mike nodded and drove off, leaving a cloud of dust behind him. Pointing to the right, up a lazy incline, Ethan announced, "the stairs are about seven miles cross-country that way."

Eric twirled his machete and said, "good thing I brought this."

Hiking off the trail was much different than on the trail, like driving through town versus riding a bike through town. Not only was it more difficult and slower to trample through the fern-covered forest floor, but it felt more adventurous, more rugged.

Normally, Ethan wouldn't go more than a few hundred feet from a trail, it just wasn't safe, but getting lost wasn't really a top concern in a forest that was out to kill hikers like him, especially considering Ethan's tenacity for navigation.

As for the forest itself, nothing about it felt off. The whispering still hadn't begun, though that was likely to change soon, and there were no signs of paranormal activity like last weekend. An intrusive thought crept into Ethan's mind, *what if the stairs aren't real, and I just hallucinated?*

There was no hallucination, however. After hours of hiking, night fell, and the whispering assaulted their ears once again.

"That is so damn frustrating!" Eric hissed, "I just can't tell what it's saying."

Looking forward blankly, Alex said, "just wait until we get closer, maybe it will be clearer then."

"Don't ignore the whispering now, though," Ethan said, "it has to be important."

Soon enough, they linked up with the trail from before. Ethan stopped and stepped into one of the boot prints in the dusty trail. It fit perfectly. "It's this way, guys," he said, although he didn't need to check the print. They could have determined that based on the direction of the eerie whispering.

The clearing was the same as it was a week ago. The stairs stood ominously in the center and the whispering pounded against Ethan's ears. He still couldn't understand what they were saying.

Again, they circled the structure, but even inches from the drywall on the side, the whispering became no clearer. "I think I'm going to have to climb them," Eric said.

Ethan nodded in response, following Eric and Alex back around to the first step. For a moment, Eric stood still and stared at the step. It still boggled Ethan's mind how out of place it was. Carpet in the woods! He would have laughed if he weren't terrified.

Eric lifted his boot to the first step, dirtying the white carpet. He yanked it back, gasping.

"What is it?" Ethan hissed.

"I… uh... never mind," Eric stammered and stepped back onto it, with both feet this time. He slowly climbed the next four, and his mouth began to move. Ethan was no lip reader, but it looked like Eric was mumbling nonsense under his breath.

"What are you trying to say?" Eric groaned. In a burst of speed, he leapt forward, taking two or three steps at a time until he was only a few from the top. Eric screamed.

Clutching at his left arm, he tumbled off the stairs. It looked like something shoved him off, but nothing else was on the stairs. He fell ten feet to the wild grass below. He landed with a thud, and a puff of dust marked his impact.

"What happened?" Ethan shouted, running with Alex towards Eric. Eric remained motionless on the ground, struggling to catch his breath. Kneeling at his side, Ethan reached for Eric's left arm.

His hand was gone.

It was a perfect, clean cut, right where his wrist met his hand, and there was no blood. The stump looked like it had been cauterized years ago and given a chance to heal too. If Ethan didn't know him, he would have thought that Eric lost his hand in an accident long ago.

Ethan looked up at Alex and saw his own panic mirrored in Alex's shocked face. "Where's his hand at?"

Another groan slipped out of Eric's mouth. His eyes darted about underneath his eyelids. Ethan hesitated, partially reaching an arm towards Eric, but stood up instead.

"If we can find his hand, they could reattach it at a hospital," Alex said with a thousand-yard stare.

They searched around the base of the stairs, careful not to touch them. When at first, they didn't find the severed hand, Ethan and Alex fanned out and looked through a wider area of the clearing, but still, nothing turned up.

Wind whooshed through the tall grass of the clearing. An owl called from the distance. Ethan stared back at the stairs; the whispering was gone. Eric awoke and breathed in sharply and Ethan rushed back to his side.

"What happened?"

Eric's pupils were dilated, and he kept glancing at the stairs. "When I climbed," he said, "the voices got clearer with every step. I still couldn't understand every word, but just a few more steps and it would have been clear as day." He stared at Ethan with his wide eyes, "I need to go back up. I need to hear what they're saying."

"No," Ethan said firmly, "we need to get out of here and regroup. This just complicates things."

Ethan helped Eric to his feet, then Eric ripped his arm out of Ethan's grip. He sprinted back towards the stairs. Ethan panicked, *if he goes back up there it will only make things worse!* Ethan lunged for Eric's legs, intending to tackle him. In the process, however, Ethan's nose collided with the heel of Eric's boot, and the two men went down in a puff of dust.

Snarling like an injured animal, Eric turned back on Ethan and pounced on him—to pin his shoulders, Ethan assumed. He snatched Eric's wrist and used the leverage to wrestle him onto the ground, reversing their roles.

Eric's response baffled Ethan. Sure, Eric could be abrasive and sarcastic at times, but he never meant it. This hands-on approach was not like him. Before Ethan could think what to do, an uppercut slammed into his chin. He blacked out for half a second and Eric squirmed to get away, no doubt to climb to the top of the stairs. In a moment of desperation, Ethan grabbed a stone from the ground, and smacked it into Eric's head. Eric dropped like a ragdoll.

He lay motionless. Motionless, but still breathing. And the clearing was silent.

Ethan rolled off Eric and wiped his nose on his white shirt. It left a gleaming smear of red, visible in the moonlight.

He closed his eyes and inhaled through his mouth. To Alex, he said, "we need to get out of here, use the gps to send a message that we need to get picked up asap."

Alex typed the message as he asked, "how are we going to get him out of here?"

"I'll figure something out," Ethan said, "but we should be more worried about what we do with him when we get home."

"What do you mean?"

"Based on how he just fought me," Ethan said, wiping more blood from his nose, "it's likely that he'll try to come back here. Or worse, he'll start telling people about the stairs."

"And if he tells people…" Alex said.

"Then the Forest Service will find out and assume that we plan to go public with the story. That one ranger was willing to kill us last week, I can't even imagine what they'll do if they decide that they need to silence us."

With Alex's help, Ethan fashioned a stretcher out of two long sticks and some clothes. Neither man spoke as they carried Eric out of the wilderness. It would be early morning by the time that they got back to the rendezvous point.

Ethan shuddered. He was in the middle of nowhere at nighttime, in a place where the forest ranger had already ordered him to avoid, and the shock of what just happened was wearing off, transforming into dread. The stairs just severed Eric's hand! And it wasn't just that. A hand could be cut off in a million different ways, but most of them involved blood and an expensive hospital visit to heal the wound. Eric's hand appeared to be healed already, and thankfully so.

"We can't take him to a hospital," Ethan said.

"He needs to get it checked out though, we don't know what those stairs did to him."

"How the hell would we explain that? They wouldn't believe us if we said it just happened by accident. All it will do is draw attention to us."

Alex grunted in response.

"You know," Ethan said, "we could blow the lid off this whole coverup. Go to the news or something, or even just start talking about it to other backpackers."

"Why?"

"The Forest Service obviously knows more than we do, so if there is a lot of attention on the stairs, they would have to do something about them."

"No," Alex retorted, "that wouldn't be smart. The only thing that that would do is attract more curious people to come check out the stairs, and more people would get hurt or go missing. And besides, the Forest Service would have already done something if there was anything that they could do. They might know more, but that doesn't mean that they have the ability to do anything with that information."

"Okay, you're right, we can spend some time thinking and come up with a plan later, let's just take Eric back to our house and rest first."

Chapter 7

Memories of the stairs haunted Ethan at night. In the weeks following the loss of Eric's hand, all he could think about were the stairs, and his nightmares about them were sickening. Over and over again he relived the first time that they called his name, and countless times he watched Eric lose his hand. Regardless of the many nightmares, the stairs' whispering was present in every one.

Something about it made sense. It was like he intuitively knew that they spoke the truth. But whatever that truth was, it was a sinister one. Horrible, forbidden knowledge. Ethan knew that nothing good could come from listening, but he still wanted to know with every fiber of his being.

The nightmares crept into his day to day life. In the welding shop, he had a clear view to the stairs that led to the second-floor offices. He found himself looking at them throughout the day, obsessing over the events in the forest. That, combined with his poor sleep, caused a significant decline in the quality of his work.

In the evenings, Ethan returned to his home and saw his empty backpack, sitting on the floor by his bed. Backpacking was one of Ethan's favorite activities, and he hiked into the wilderness whenever life became too overwhelming. Now, however, he couldn't even imagine going backpacking again in his life. He feared that he would wake up in the night and hear those terrible whispers again. Ethan desperately wanted to put the whole ordeal behind him, but he knew that he couldn't just let it go. He felt he had a duty to figure out what was going on. To save the unfortunate hikers that the stairs took the lives of. But now, fear was stronger than his curiosity.

On the other hand, Eric recovered swiftly after returning home. It seemed that all he needed was some rest and distance from the stairs. He managed to keep his missing hand mostly concealed, but it was getting the attention of a few people, he explained to Ethan. He remedied the situation by simply telling them to mind their own business.

| | |

On a Wednesday evening, Ethan approached Alex in the living room. Alex was playing a shooter videogame, sitting on the couch with all the lights off. "Alex, we still haven't addressed how we're going to deal with the stairs."

"Do we really need to? Only a few people have gone missing since we were there."

"I can't sleep at night. I can't go to work without obsessing over the stairs. Like it or not, we stumbled onto something bad and we have a moral obligation to do something about it."

"Ethan!" Alex said with a cynical laugh. He quit the match he was in and put down the controller, giving Ethan his full attention. "What can we do about it? I'm still not sure that what we saw up there was even real, and if it is, we have no idea what it is. We can't blow the whistle on the whole thing, either."

With his arms crossed, Ethan stood in place, thinking. He was silent for a few minutes, before he said, "we could destroy it." Destroying the stairs was the obvious response. If something is hurting the community, it must be destroyed. But it made Ethan nervous.

"Can it be destroyed?" Alex asked, "the weather didn't affect the stairs, they were in pristine condition, better than our staircase here at home."

"Do you have a better idea?"

Alex was silent again. After a few seconds of contemplation, he simply said, "no."

"We still have to hike in, so we can't bring any big tools. Maybe just some hatchets, and hammers to remove any nails if there are any."

"There is another problem," Alex added, "after Eric lost his hand, Mike told me that he wants nothing to do with our missions, so we don't have a way to get to our secret drop-off spot."

"Actually, that won't be a problem. When he was dropping us off last time, I noticed a good spot for hiding a truck. If I knew that it was there before, I wouldn't have asked him to drive us. I'm ready to go whenever, but when are you available?"

Alex checked his phone, scrolling through his busy schedule. "Well, I have a test coming up on Friday, and another on Monday morning, so how about we go on Monday evening. Can you get off work for those days?"

"I'll take care of it," Ethan said.

| | |

Standing on the dirt road in the wilderness, Ethan stared at his camouflaged truck. He went over it repeatedly, scrutinizing his work. In a few spots, the grey paint was visible from the road, but it matched the day's overcast sky, so Ethan felt comfortable leaving his truck there—to someone that didn't know where to look, it would be invisible.

It was Monday evening. Ethan and Alex drove to the secret parking spot after Alex returned home from taking his exam. With them they each brought a hatchet and a hammer, and Ethan even took a small bottle of lighter fluid. Alex told him not to bring it. He said that if the tools didn't work on the stairs, then fire wouldn't either, but Ethan still held out hope that burning the stairs as a last resort would work. Ethan knew that fire was a powerful weapon against creatures like Skinwalkers and Wendigos.

Once they arrived, Ethan parked his truck in the little pullout that he noticed before, and then spent the next half hour using fallen limbs and bits of ferns to hide his truck from any prying eyes that might drive by on the road.

"If I didn't know it was there," Alex said, "I wouldn't be able to see it."

Satisfied with his work, Ethan smiled, donned his pack, and said, "let's go do some demolition."

Carrying the means to destroy the stairs was empowering for Ethan. Now that he was no longer afraid, hiking through this part of the forest was starting to get tedious. Ethan took a swig from his water bottle and quickened his pace. *The third time's the charm, I guess*, he thought. It felt like the hike went by quicker this time, and they arrived at the stairs well before sunset.

The staircase was still quite ominous. It cast a long shadow, nearly to the edge of the clearing, and the forest was unnaturally silent in the area. Ethan pulled his hatchet from a loop on his pack, brandishing the head at his side. He dropped his pack to the ground. The stairs remained silent. Ethan treaded towards it and stopped a few feet away from the side. He lifted his hatchet to shoulder height but did not swing yet.

He turned to look at Alex, who nodded his affirmation. Ethan swung the steel blade with all his weight, and it smashed into the stairs. The second his hatchet collided with the cream-colored drywall, a flash of blue light blinded Ethan. Then he felt weightless. A shockwave roared into his ears; it was one of the loudest things he had ever heard. Soon, the blast was replaced by the sound of rushing wind as Ethan was thrown through the air. Still blind, he crashed into the ground. Hard. His breath escaped him, and he writhed in the dirt, begging his diaphragm to start working again. A handful of grim moments went by and Ethan managed to take a few short breaths again.

Looking up, the trees on the rim of the clearing still shook from the shockwave of whatever threw Ethan. Alex was on his hands and knees. Ethan got to his feet, scraped up and bleeding from the fall.

"What the hell…" he muttered to himself. He was halfway between the stairs in the center, and the trees on the edge. Ethan coughed and spat out a glob of blood. By then, Alex was on his feet, cautiously stepping backwards, his expression one of fear.

Ethan regarded the stairs in a new light. He stared at them, considering the kind of power it would take to throw a nearly two-hundred-pound man like Ethan. Of course, he still feared the nefarious structure, but no longer was that the only emotion that the sight of them evoked. He was in awe.

"Alex!" he shouted, "come over here. Let's check out the damage."

"No man, I'm not going near those anymore."

Ethan stroll towards the stairs again and tapped on their side with his index finger. "See," he said, "they only throw you when you hurt them."

Alex took a few nervous steps forward. "Where's your hatchet?" he asked.

"I hadn't even thought about that." He scanned the clearing where he fell, but he saw no sign of it. In the tree line, however, there was a glint of light about four feet in the air. Approaching it, Ethan realized that it was his hatchet, embedded two inches deep into a snag. He pulled it out, creating a wet crackling sound as he ripped free a chunk of rotting wood with it.

"I'm glad that didn't fly off and hit me," Alex said.

Ethan gave him a surprised look, raising both of his eyebrows. "Let's go see what I did to the stairs," he said, turning to walk back to the malevolent structure.

Both examined the spot where he struck the stairs. Nothing. The structure was completely undamaged. "Back up," Ethan said, "I want to try something else."

Once Ethan and Alex were a sufficient distance away, Ethan lifted his hatchet above his head and threw it like a tomahawk at the stairs. It sailed through the air silently. On impact, there was another blinding flash of light, emanating from the point of impact, and the sound of a detonation echoed through the mountains. The hatchet shot nearly straight upwards, before careening back down and embedding itself in the dirt.

"This isn't working," Alex said.

"One more thing," Ethan said while reaching into his pack. He produced the can of lighter fluid and a book of matches.

"Come on, Ethan, that's stupid," Alex chided, "what if you start a forest fire? If it reacts badly to a hatchet, who knows what it will do if you try to light it on fire?"

Ethan hesitated. "No," he said, "fire is different, it won't react violently."

"How do you know that?"

"I just have a feeling," Ethan said, approaching the stairs. He squirted a generous amount of the fluid on the first step, soaking the once-pristine carpeting. He lit a match and dropped it onto the soiled fabric. It didn't light. He lit another match. Still nothing. Confused, Ethan rubbed his fingers on the wet patch, then brought them back up to his nose. The liquid no longer smelled of lighter fluid, and it no longer had its consistency.

"Alex, this is weird, you have to come check this out."

"What is it?"

"When I poured the fluid on, the stairs turned it into water, and it didn't light."

Shaking his head, Alex said, "I told you fire wouldn't work."

"But it didn't fight back like it did when I hit it with the hatchet."

"Okay then—" Alex stopped midsentence. Voices echoed through the trees in the distance. They sounded angry. Ethan thought about the ranger that stopped them. It seemed impossible for one man to track them for so long, but what if it wasn't one man? It was certainly possible, if they so desperately wanted to keep the stairs a secret, the Forest Service would put many sentries in the forest surrounding the stairs.

"Those blasts were making a lot of noise," Alex said, looking at Ethan with horror in his eyes.

Ethan whispered, "run back to the truck, hopefully they won't think to track us off trail."

They sprinted out of the clearing, thrashing through thick brush. Ethan cut himself on various branches and brush as he rushed through the forest. He didn't care. The back of his neck tingled, and he couldn't help but imagine the sound of a hunting rifle firing, followed by a hot bullet striking him in the back.

Thinking that made his back itch.

"They must be using the stairs for something," Ethan shouted over the wind, "maybe they found some way to take advantage of their power and are trying to keep it all to themselves."

"If that was the case, then why were there no guards in the clearing?"

"Then it has to be something else," Ethan said. "If the stairs become public knowledge, then they would have to deal with them directly, and they don't want to do that."

"They're afraid," Alex concluded.

Somehow, that was worse. Selfish people were to be expected, but dealing with scared people was more dangerous. They could react violently, like a drowning person sacrificing their rescuer to get their head above water.

It was dark when they arrived at Ethan's truck. And they were tired. After fleeing seven miles through rough terrain, Ethan was too exhausted to keep his guard up fully. He sighed, sluggishly pulling the brush off his truck. "This hike is getting tedious," he said.

Ethan whipped out of the pullout and drove eastbound, just a little bit too fast, desperate to get home and out of this horrible forest. In the dark, driving was much more dangerous than during the day. With roads as untraveled as these, none of the turns were marked with chevrons, and the roads weren't named; they were numbered. It wasn't very conducive to easy navigation. Ethan pushed on though, winding through the labyrinth.

Headlights lit up Ethan's rearview mirror. He slammed his foot on the gas pedal, throwing out any regard for safety.

"What are you doing, Ethan?" Alex screamed, "these roads aren't designed for you to go this fast!"

The speedometer passed forty. The truck behind him sped up. Ethan felt his heart skip a beat, and gravel flew into the air when Ethan took a turn too quick. Luckily, he didn't go off the road, but he totally lost control of the truck. It spun around once, so that it faced their pursuers, with the tailgate pressed into a thick Douglas Fir. The other truck slowed down and came to a stop just inches away from Ethan's grill, using its armored front bumper to lock Ethan's truck in place. He was trapped.

Defeated, Ethan turned the key and the engine went silent. With his window opened, he could smell the putrid stench of burnt rubber. Before he could react, the other truck's lights switched off, and car doors slammed. Ethan watched a dark figure approach his window.

Raising his left arm in a weak attempt at defense, Ethan was powerless to stop the man. He punched Ethan right on the cheek bone, and Ethan folded in his seat like a dead fish. One of his teeth popped loose. His head slammed into the steering wheel, and Ethan passed out to the fading sound of his blaring, monotone horn.

| | |

What makes reality real? If Plato was right, nothing does, and reality is subjective. In his unconscious state, Ethan passively considered the idea. He imagined that all his experiences with the stairs were all part of a twisted fever dream, and he was still swinging in his hammock on the first expedition—without the whispering.

The analytical part of his mind kept telling him that the stairs were real, and they had a rational explanation. His superstitious side told him that he made the mistake of trifling with an ancient, elder god. In his heart, though, he just wanted to sleep.

Then the whispering disturbed him in his hammock, and it started swaying uncontrollably. But he could understand it this time!

"We're almost at the lookout," a deep male voice said.

"Good," another, higher pitched, but still deep, voice said matter-of-factly.

In the dream, the hammock underneath him shifted, and he was sitting upright, then it morphed into a car seat. And reality returned. Ethan groaned. Memories of the past evening flooded his mind, and he gasped. Ethan opened his eyes to blackness, and felt fabric wrapped around his face. *I've been kidnapped!* he remembered. His head hurt too.

Ethan struggled and discovered that he could not move. His hands were bound behind his back and his feet were tied together.

"He's waking up," a third voice said. It came directly from Ethan's right.

Realizing that there was nothing he could do now, Ethan sat and listened. The vehicle he was riding in was hitting plenty of bumps and potholes and shaking from side to side.

They were on a rough road, if not completely off road. And Ethan's back pressed into the seat more than normal, so they must have been going uphill. What was it that the one man said earlier? Something about a lookout. That had to be important, but Ethan's splitting headache prevented him from connecting the dots, so he filed away the information to be analyzed later.

The truck rolled to a stop, crunching gravel beneath its tires, and the door to Ethan's left swung open. Someone unbuckled his seatbelt and yanked him out of the truck. He stumbled on his stiff legs, but a strong hand gripped his bicep and prevented a fall. As best as he could tell through the thick fabric obscuring his vision, it was still nighttime.

The grip on his arm remained, and it led Ethan away from the truck. He heard Alex grumbling from behind him.

"Staircase up ahead, watch your step."

What? Were they going to execute him on the stairs? Ethan roared and kicked, fighting against his captors. He whipped his head back and it collided with a man's face. Cartilage snapped. Another man rushed to the aid of the one holding Ethan, and the two men kicked him to the ground.

"Calm down dumbass, they're not *those* stairs!"

Ethan grumbled his submission and let them take him up the staircase. It creaked and was made of wood. At the top, one of the men dug some keys out of his pocket and unlocked a door. Once inside, they kicked the back of Ethan's knees, knocking him to the floor. A thud next to him told him that the same was done to Alex.

"Let them sleep for now," one of the voices said, "we'll figure out what to do with them in the morning."

Ethan wanted to resist. To fight his captors and run off into the night. But his pounding headache made sleep an incredibly attractive offer. And he had no idea where he was. Even if he could escape, where would he go? No, he would take the opportunity to rest, and act in the morning.

Chapter 8

When Ethan was young, his family rented a fire lookout for a weekend getaway. It was one of those isolate buildings, on stilts tens of feet in the air on top of a mountain. They used to be manned year-round by lookouts so that forest fires could be identified and stopped. With new technology, however, they started to get phased out of use over the years. The lookouts all had beautiful views and were sitting with no use, so many were auctioned off or used as rentals.

Not all of them were sold, apparently. Ethan awoke to the panoramic glass windows that peered out across the rolling hills of the coast range for miles in every direction. With minimal insulation and no heating system, cold morning air chilled Ethan's skin. He wished that he brought a hoodie when he went to destroy the stairs. The stairs! Yesterday's memories came flooding back, and a spike of adrenaline terrorized Ethan's stomach. Alex was still asleep, about five feet away from Ethan on the floor. He searched the one-room structure for his kidnappers.

One man sat on the opposite corner of the room with his chin tucked into his neck. He huddled next to a small woodstove. Only a few coals were still smoldering within it. Ethan struggled against his bonds and managed to sit up. He winced in pain. The movement reopened countless scabs he earned by running through the forest yesterday.

In a fit of coughing, the man by the stove woke up. He looked at Ethan like a deer in the headlights. "The others will be back soon," he said.

The man wore a tan and dark green outfit and had a badge on his shirt. "Why are you trying to hide the stairs," Ethan demanded. The Forest Ranger bowed his head, ignoring him. "I can tell that you work for the Forest Service, and I know that you guys are covering something up."

Ethan jeered at the Ranger for another few minutes but failed to get a rise out of him. He gave up and entertained himself by staring out the windows of the lookout.

Ethan was studying a hawk perched on a snag when a truck parked in front of the fire lookout. It came tearing up the long, winding driveway then scraped to a stop, spitting gravel. Ethan held his breath. Car doors slammed and two sets of footsteps climbed the stairs to the room. Two men strode in, surveying Ethan and Alex with disgust in their eyes. One man's nose was swollen to a ridiculous size with cotton stuffed into his nostrils. He sneered at Ethan.

The other man asked, "any trouble while we were gone, Mason?"

"No sir, that one only woke up a moment ago," the man—Mason, apparently—said while pointing at Ethan.

"*That one* deserves a beating before we put him down," the man with the broken nose said. Ethan recognized his deep voice from last night, but now it was nasally too.

"You'll get a chance for that," the other man said. Ethan was beginning to think that this one was in charge.

The leader approached Ethan, putting his hands on his hips and chewing on his lip. "You have certainly caused us a lot of trouble, and you know too much ab—"

"about how you're afraid to confront the stairs," Ethan interrupted.

The leader's lip twitched, and he narrowed his eyes dangerously, the first sign of anger that he had shown. "You have no idea what you're talking about," he sneered. He reached behind his back, then produced a small handgun. "You know too much about something you should never have discovered, and now I have to get rid of you for it." He pulled back the hammer. Ethan scrambled backwards as best he could while tied up, but the leader pressed the barrel of the gun to his forehead.

"Wait! Wait!" he screamed, "There's something you should know!" The leader frowned but took his finger off the trigger. Ethan still felt the cold steel against his skin. "One of my friends also knows what we know, and he climbed the stairs too. He lost his hand! And if we go missing, he's going to blow the lid off your whole operation!"

The leader pursed his lips and turned his back on Ethan. "God dammit," he cursed. Pointing at Mason, he ordered, "stay here and make sure they don't try anything." Then they left as quickly as he arrived. Ethan listened in victory to the sound of a truck barreling down the mountain, spraying dirt and gravel as it raced away. He smiled despite his grim situation.

"Why are you smiling?" Mason asked, "he's going to kill your friend now."

"What? No, he won't, I didn't tell him anything about who my friend is."

"You didn't tell him *Ethan*, but your license plate did." Ethan's heart dropped, and he felt a burst of adrenaline. *He knows my name*! As if he read Ethan's mind, Mason Continued, "yeah, it didn't take much digging to find out who you are and who you hang around with."

Ethan sneered. "And now you're gloating? Fuck you!"

"I'm not gloating, I wish that you didn't get yourself into this mess."

"If you really cared, you wouldn't be working for them, then!"

Mason stopped. "I didn't know it would be like this when I signed up."

"What?" Ethan asked, leaning forward. "Then why do you still work for them?"

Mason looked at his feet. "For one, I need the money, but… I really believe in the ideals of the organization, and I don't want to leave it just because it's run by cowards."

Ethan saw an opportunity. "Then change that," he said, "let me out of these zip ties and we can work together."

Mason fiddled with his hands nervously. "Work together on what?"

"Destroying the stairs."

"No, it can't be done."

"How do you know?"

"The higher-ups in the Forest Service have more information on these things than you can even imagine. They haven't told me much, but they are sure that the stairs cannot be destroyed under any circumstances."

"Then we can work together to steal the information that they haven't shared with you yet!" Ethan shifted his position slightly and felt something on the floor scrape his hand. It was a nail. Partially pulled out from the floorboards, the steel was at just the right angle that Ethan could use it to break the zip tie around his wrists. He would have to be fast, though; Mason would realize the second he broke the tie, so Ethan would have to lunge at him the second he was freed. *I hope he doesn't have a gun.*

"Stop trying to get into my head," Mason said halfheartedly, "I'm not helping you."

Ethan had more trouble than he thought he would, using the nail to break the tie. It kept slipping off and he couldn't put enough pressure on before he became too worried that Mason would notice. After a few stressful seconds, he snapped his zip tie. Ethan froze. He held both of his hands in the air to his sides. He met Mason's eyes, and neither man moved.

Ethan lunged. He awkwardly pushed himself to his feet and jumped with both in the same point—it wasn't like he could get better footing. Mason shouted a moment before Ethan smashed into him. They tumbled to the floor and Ethan scraped his arm on the iron woodstove. He grunted then ignored the pain. They scuffled for a few more moments, and Ethan even gained the upper hand once or twice, but ultimately, he was at a disadvantage. Mason pinned him.

Although he couldn't see much other than Mason's face, he heard Alex squirming and grunting behind him. The fight must have woken him up. Mason's face was painted with a confusing mix of emotions. Mainly, there was shock, and a primal sneer of ferocity. But there was also something else: confusion. No, betrayal. *Maybe if I just try talking to him a bit more*—Mason pulled out a gun. *Shit*.

It was of a similar make as the leader's, and the barrel was just as cold against Ethan's neck. Ethan stared into the ranger's eyes and saw nothing but fear. "You won't kill me," Ethan said, "you don't have it in you. Drop the act, I know you don't want to keep taking orders from that asshole."

Mason's hand started shaking, and the barrel of the gun quivered against Ethan's neck. "How can I trust you?" he demanded with a shaky voice.

"Because we have two common enemies: the stairs, and the Forest Service."

Mason squeezed his eyes shut, as if he were fighting an inner demon. "Fine," he gasped, taking the gun off Ethan's neck. It clattered to the floor. With his hands now free, Ethan got his pocketknife and cut free the ties on his ankles.

"How long until they get back here?" Ethan asked.

"Hours at the least," Mason muttered, "it will take a while to track down your friend."

Picking up the gun, Ethan asked, "and how do I save him?"

Mason scoffed. "Get out of here. The only way they won't just shoot him in the back of the head like they already tried to do to you is if they know you are still out there to blow the whistle."

Ethan cut Alex free from his zip ties. "Well let's start here," Ethan said, "what do *you* know about the stairs."

"Not much," Mason started, "they don't exactly cover it in orientation. Mainly, what I know is from bits of information I've picked up over the three years of working for the Forest Service. Once I started, it took months before I even saw the things. Me and another, older ranger were assisting with a search and rescue mission when we encountered one set of stairs. They—"

"There are multiple staircases?"

"Obviously," Mason continued, annoyed by the interruption. "Anyway, this staircase looked like it was from Ancient Rome. Pristine white marble. And it was wide, too. I flipped out, because it made no sense, and the other forest ranger basically told me that they were normal in this area and to never go near them. I was so shocked the next day that I wasn't sure if I was remembering correctly, but I took his advice to heart."

"As I saw more and more of them over the years," Mason said, "I started asking more questions. That's when I got what we call 'the talk,' where they explained how the stairs lure in and kill people. More importantly, they told me to never speak about them, and that they were the Forest Service's greatest secret."

"You do know," Ethan interjected, "that they won't let you speak about them because they are afraid of facing the problem."

"Again, obviously," Mason said, perturbed.

"We plan on facing the problem," Ethan explained. Alex nodded resolutely. "Will you join us?"

Mason didn't answer.

"If you don't, and you stay here, they might kill you."

Grinding his teeth for a second, Mason finally said, "okay, I'm in. What's the plan?"

"You said that the older ranger told you not to worry? That means that someone in the Forest Service knows all about the stairs, so we need to find them and interrogate them."

"I have a better plan," Mason smirked a little. "There is a small ranger station that they use for storage. They don't waste resources on guards because, officially, there isn't anything important inside the station. But the big rumor is, that's just to keep heat off the station, and they actually use it to store artifacts related to the stairs."

"There are artifacts?"

"Ethan, you have no idea how big this conspiracy is."

"Then let's find out. Do you know how to get to this station?"

"Yeah, we can take my truck. It's a bit old, but it will get us where we need to go."

Ethan didn't even think about transport, he was lucky that Mason had a truck here. "Okay, let's go, we don't have any time to waste. The faster we figure out what to do next, the sooner we can help Eric."

"Let's destroy these fucking stairs," Alex said.

Mason's truck was old. Like forty years old. Still, it beat walking. For the first time, Ethan got to see the road that brought him to the lookout. He already knew that it was gravel and unkempt. He heard that much. What surprised him was how narrow it was. Where it connected to a more travelled road at the bottom, it could even be confused as a bike path by an untrained eye. It was that unnoticeable. The truck pushed through a wall of maple leaves as Mason put them on the road, and Ethan realized now how good of a spot that fire lookout was to kill somebody.

"So, Ethan, I'm curious," Mason said, keeping his eyes on the road. "How did you discover the stairs? The Forest Service spends a ridiculous amount of resources on keeping them secret."

"Actually, it was Alex that first discovered something was wrong."

"What?" Alex asked, startled. "Someone said my name, I wasn't paying attention."

"I was explaining to Mason that your discovery led us to find the stairs."

"Oh yeah," said Alex, "with the increasing disappearances, your explanation about the cougars didn't match up. Ethan and I talked about it and decided that you guys were probably hiding something."

"Coverups are really hard to pull off," Ethan said. "Maybe we should give conspiracy theorists more credit."

"Hmmm."

Chapter 9

The ranger station was only one building. It had a slanted roof that was split by a cobbled stone chimney. Mason pulled off the highway, onto the driveway of the station. No lights were on, and it looked like it hadn't been cleaned or repainted in decades.

"See," Mason said, "low profile."

A rush of vertigo hit Ethan like a truck. Something didn't seem right. Maybe just because this was his last and only option, and the only place that held the hope of saving Eric and Destroying the stairs. But he knew that if they didn't find anything…

Mason produced a key and unlocked the door to the ranger station. "Most of the keys are standardized," he said, "which is really convenient for us."

Inside were stacks of boxes and nondescript piles of papers. A few shovels stood in the corner of the entryway. Cobwebs cluttered the room, and dirt was strewn on the floor. Ethan picked up a packet from a box on his left. It was an expense report for a landscaping job. Ethan yawned. "Is the whole place like this," he asked.

"Yeah, that's the point. We'll just need to do some searching around to find something that could help us." Mason flicked a light switch, and a gross yellow color illuminated the room. Leaving the entryway, Mason led them into what could be considered a living room, but it was decorated just as poorly as the entryway: stacks and stacks of useless papers and junk. "Okay, guys, let's split up and search the station. Look for anything out of the ordinary."

That was easier said than done. The whole station was the epitome of boredom. The most interesting thing that Ethan had seen so far was a spot of rust on a hammer. He opened a box. Papers. He opened another. More documents. Alex and Mason were doing the same, so Ethan decided to stop with the boxes. They could search through the cardboard cubes all day long and still find nothing.

Something about all the boxes and papers felt wrong to Ethan. He picked up another and examined the date. It was a payroll report from 1972! What could the Forest Service possibly need that for? And if they were truly worried about keeping it, why would it be here and not in some Federal database? These documents were just fodder placed to distract from something else.

"Guys," Ethan said, "stop checking the boxes. They're just a distraction. The real prize has to be somewhere else."

"Does this place have an attic?" Alex asked.

"I would assume so, let's see what we can find," Mason said.

The attic was tucked away in a closet with a pull-down staircase. If his situation weren't so dire, Ethan would have laughed at the irony. One by one, they climbed into the attic, Ethan taking point. Unlike the rest of the building, it was empty. Completely empty. It had nothing but pink, fiberglass insulation. But most buildings have their furnaces in the attic.

"Shit," Ethan said, pushing his way past Mason and Alex to go back down the stairs.

"Where are you going," Alex asked, "we haven't even looked around up here."

"You two do that, I need to check something." Ethan rushed out the front door and did a quick circle around the house. He was right. There was no external furnace, and no external air conditioning unit either. He rushed back inside.

In the living room he approached a vent in the floor. "Guys! Come here!"

"What is it?" the other two asked simultaneously.

"I think I found something." They came running. "This building has neither heating or A/C."

"So what?" Alex asked.

Ethan pointed at the vent. "Then why would it have that?"

"Wait," Mason said, eyes widening, "you think they are hiding things…"

"Yes, in the old HVAC system." Ethan pulled his knife from his pocket and used it as a makeshift screwdriver, removing the vent cover. With the screws out, the metal piece came out easily. Still, Ethan didn't see anything down there.

"See anything?" Mason asked.

"Give me a second." Ethan plunged his left arm down the hole. After about a foot and a half it curved and ran parallel with the floor. He followed the bend, but still felt nothing. Ethan laid down all the way and went shoulder-deep into the vent. His fingertips touched something. It felt like paper, but it was soft and floppy. *Not more documents*, he thought.

He grabbed the stack and yanked it out of the vent. "You have *got* to be kidding me!" Ethan shouted, throwing the papers against the wall.

"No, wait," Alex said, "look at these." He pointed at the headlines of newspaper stories that were clipped out. They were all missing persons stories. "I think we're onto something, see if there is anything else."

Ethan obeyed, digging deeper into the pipe. He pushed as hard as he could, and felt the floorboards cut into his shoulder. Another stack of newspaper clippings came out.

Mason stared in awe. "All of these people were killed by the stairs?"

Although it was a rhetorical question, Ethan responded cynically, "let's hope so, that would mean we just hit the jackpot for information."

But the jackpot wasn't in the vent. Ethan plunged his arm in again and turned up nothing. Mason and Alex both insisted that they double check too, but neither was able to reach anything.

"Okay, let's check the other rooms. If these newspaper clippings are the only things of value, this was a waste," Ethan said.

He entered a room adjacent to the living room. The large desk in the middle of the room suggested that it might have been an office once, but the same stacks of boxes and miscellaneous tools scattered around the room made it hard to be sure. Ethan checked the drawers of the desk, but all were empty.

Ethan was about to leave the room, but a glint of light caught his eye from underneath the empty desk. He pushed the desk out of the way. Sitting before him on the floor was the flat face of inground safe.

Chapter 10

"I found the real jackpot, guys," Ethan called. Alex and Mason rushed into the room. Ethan gestured at the safe in the ground. It's thick, square face was flush with the hardwood floor. Within the square of metal was a circle whose vertices contacted the side of the square. There were hinges on one side of the circle. A small keyhole occupied the side of the circle opposite its hinges; that would open the circular hatch.

"Is it unlocked?" Alex asked.

"Let me try some of my keys," Mason said. He kneeled before the safe and tried his many keys on the lock. None of them worked, but Ethan wasn't surprised. "Do either of you know how to pick locks?"

"I think Mike does, but he isn't here," Alex said.

"That's ironic," Ethan remarked.

"Well then we need to break into it," Mason said.

Ethan tapped the thick steel face of the safe. "No, you would need an acetylene torch at the minimum to get into this thing." Ethan tilted his head, looking at the hinges of the safe. "Unless…" he said, "guys, go grab some hammers and some axes, there have to be some in this place. If we can get it out of the floor, I have an idea."

They spent the next hour hacking at the floorboards. It was easier than Ethan thought it would be. Whoever put the safe in was lazy enough that they only attached it to the floorboards at the top. It hung free in the crawl space without bottom braces or concrete.

The last bolt, however, gave Mason some trouble coming out, and he muttered something under his breath. At the intonation, Ethan flinched. It sounded like whispering.

Finally, the safe came free of its basement prison. Ethan picked up the heavy cube, grunting in exertion as he did so, and he shook it. He felt something moving around inside, but it either wasn't very heavy, or it wasn't awfully hard. Something that wouldn't normally be kept in a super secure safe.

"Okay, Ethan, how do you plan on getting this open?" Alex asked.

"I'm going to jam the claw of a hammer into the side of the safe, where the hinges are, and drive the Mason's truck onto the handle. It should pry open the safe."

"I don't like that," Mason said, "what if something goes wrong and you pop my tire? I don't have a spare."

"Do you have any other ideas?"

"We could cut it open."

"With what tools?"

Mason frowned and tapped his fingers against his leg. After a few moments, "yeah, I guess you're right, we don't have an option."

"Okay, fire up the truck," said Ethan. Ethan wiggled his hammer's claw into the crack between the safe's two hinges. It was at an angle so that the truck's weight would pop it right open when the tire drove over.

He carried it with both arms. It wasn't too heavy, but the cumbersome shape didn't make it easy to hold. Alex opened the door for him while Mason ran out to start up the truck.

Setting the safe on the ground by the truck's front tire, Ethan tapped the hood and commanded, "take it slow, I'll tell you to stop if anything shifts out of place."

Mason inched the truck forward. It reminded Ethan of the slow movements his Grandfather taught him to do when hitching a trailer. The brakes whined and squeaked from the tiny movements. When the tire was just inches away, Mason stopped, and Ethan gave him a thumbs up. He drove forward, transferring the weight of the truck onto the handle of the hammer. After a few tense moments of suspense, Mason's truck overwhelmed the hinges and the door popped free.

"You're good!" Ethan called, rushing to the open safe. After Mason backed the truck up, Ethan set the safe up right again and peered inside. It was empty. No, it wasn't, Ethan took a second look. The only item inside was a tattered, leather-bound journal that blended in with the bottom of the safe. He pulled it out. The front was unmarked, but flipping inside to the first page, it read: *April 2ⁿᵈ, 1849*. Ethan reconsidered the item in his hand. Did the disappearances go back that far?

"What is it?" Mason asked, turning off the truck.

"It's a journal from the 1849!"

"That's when the Oregon Trail happened, right?"

"Yeah, I think so."

"Let's take it inside, you can read it to Alex and I."

Ethan closed the journal and walked towards the open front door, holding the small, leather book close to his chest, as if his life depended on it. But it wasn't his life that hung in the balance, it was Eric's

They sat in a circle on the floor—the station had no furniture other than the desk—next to a large back window. Ethan opened the journal again and began reading.

"April 2nd, 1849. My name is James Walker. In this year of 1849, I have lived for twenty-eight years. Today is the day that I depart Independence, Missouri, with my wagon train to Oregon. I have decided to keep this journal to document my experiences on this journey."

Ethan skipped through many pages. "I don't think we'll learn anything of value from the trail. I'm guessing that their arrival has something to do with the stairs, though."

He flipped through page after page of filler. James wrote about his experiences and challenges along the way, but none of it was new to Ethan. The Oregon Trail was standard curriculum in school, and there was no mention of the stairs until later in the journal.

"September 19th, 1849. Today, we crossed the Snake River, and shall arrive in the Willamette valley in just a few weeks. After months of arduous travel, it is a relief to finally be so close."

They were close, but still there was no mention of the stairs. Ethan flipped ahead. "September 27th, 1849. While I was sleeping in my bedroll yesterday, a wind whipped through our camp. It was strange, as yesterday had been a clear, fair-weathered day. Yet it was not truly wind. As I listened to it, I began to hear voices. I could not hear what they were saying, but they were, without a doubt, saying something. Today, there is much work to do, and I fear that the whispering may be an Indian trick, so I will investigate tomorrow."

"The whispering!" Alex said, leaning forward with wide eyes, "This journal could have the information we need!"

"I hope so," Mason added.

"September 28th, 1849. I located the source of the mystical whispering today. A staircase has been constructed in the woods. I am not sure of its origins, but it does not appear to be of Indian construction. It is made almost completely out of iron, and is in a spiral formation, like the staircases within the great lighthouses of the East Coast. I studied it for some time, but it gave me a chilling feeling."

"For the next few days, I must help with the construction of cabins. Winter is approaching fast, and I would not like to spend it sleeping outside. I will update this journal when I have the time to revisit the staircase. Hopefully, I can convince some others to come with me. Maybe they will climb it."

"October 5th, 1849. Today I had a chance to slip away from my responsibilities at camp. For the days since my last entry I have done nothing but think about the stairs. More importantly, I've been obsessed with the whispering, and what it means. One man came with me. I cannot remember his name. He chose to climb the stairs, as it seemed that the intoxicating effect of the whispering affected him tenfold the effect it had on myself. The entire time he ascended the spiral staircase, he mumbled about the whispering getting clearer. Then he paused three quarters of the way up. He tumbled over the railing, screaming, and when he landed, one of his arms was missing."

"I could not believe my eyes, yet I was still drawn in by the stairs. What had he heard? What was it like when the injury occurred? Alas, he was knocked unconscious by the fall, and thus, I returned him to camp. I was met with suspicion and was nearly banished. I promised to take more men with me in the coming days, to prove that I was not lying about the accident."

"October 9th, 1849. I took two men to the staircase today. One of them was like me, and he resisted the call of the whispering, but the other was different. Almost immediately he took flight towards the staircase and rushed to the top without pause. When he reached the top, he screamed, 'I finally understand!' Then he vanished. There was no sound or sight, one moment he was at the top, and in another he was gone."

"I fear I have trifled with powers that should have been left alone. When we explained it to the group tonight, many believed it was a sign from God. They say that the man was called up from the staircase, and he left our mortal world for Heaven. A large group plans on going to climb the staircase tomorrow. Not all of us, but many. I am not one of them. The whispering is unholy, but they won't listen to me. Oh well, so be it. There is nothing more I can do to convince them to stay away."

"October 10th, 1849. Forty-two people disappeared on the stairs today. This morning, while I was still sleeping, fifty-seven left for the stairs, and only fifteen returned. And those that returned are in a state of disrepair, rambling nonsense and refusing to work. In the hours since they have returned, all that they have done is sit and whisper to themselves, shout aimlessly into the wind, and pace in circles. There is no sign of the people that they once were."

The handwriting of the journal was no longer neat and compact. Starting on the next entry it was rushed and messy.

The page had a few rips, as if the writer were in distress while making the entry. "October 12th, 1849. A madness has taken over the group! It must be that damned staircase! First, it was the fifteen people that returned from its heights. Yesterday they switched from rambling to acts of violence. It came as a surprise, but with our greater numbers we were able to defeat them. All of yesterday was spent fighting or burying bodies, that is why I have not written until now. We lost too many good people."

"But today, more people started rambling in the morning. Then they became violent. We tried fighting, but too many became deranged, and only a few of us remained normal. I have become separated from them. There is a chance that I will fall to their misguided hands, so I am writing this entry to warn anyone that is reading this: STAY AWAY FROM THE STAIRS AND ANYONE WHO CLIMBS THEM! I'm running through the forest right now. I think I will climb one of the fir trees and spend a night high in the air. If I survive the next few days, I will search for answers."

Turning the page, Ethan was appalled by the new state of the writing. Even the messy scratches of the last page seemed neat now. Words and letters were missing in many places, and the handwriting was barely legible. Ethan read the journal aloud as best he could, filling in the blanks for Alex and Mason. "October 13th, 1849. I climbed the stairs. I listened. I understand now. How the stairs work, that is. My sanity is fading quickly, and I don't have much time to do what I must, but I am going to explain as best I can how they work. If I fail to defeat *him*, this information will help you succeed where I failed. Oh, that's right, you don't know who *he* is."

Ethan paused from his reading. He squinted at the page. "It's like this guy went crazy, I can barely read his handwriting."

"He did climb the stairs and survive," Alex said, "keep reading, it's getting interesting."

Ethan continued reading, "There are many staircases across the Oregon Territory, and they are all linked together. They whisper ancient, forbidden knowledge in tones quiet enough that it is impossible to understand from anywhere but the top of the stairs. It doesn't matter. The knowledge contained within the whispering voices is entrancing, even when one cannot understand it, we are drawn to it. The knowledge is bait."

"When a man climbs the stairs, one of three things can happen: he will lose a limb, he will vanish, or he will survive, but with a twisted mind. The latter happened to me. When the limbs are severed, or the people vanish, they are taken to a central location. The demon named Inferius lives there. *He* feeds on them. Not physically, however, their life force is drained. That force is used to seed havoc in our world, it was what caused the insanity of my people. But I am sure that there is much more to come."

"This central location I am speaking of has the only descending staircase, but it does not stay in the same place, and it takes up no volume. I do not understand it, but I know it is true. The whispering had a word for it that I could not understand: a pocket dimension. Maybe that means something to whoever may be reading this in the future."

"I am going to find it. When I came down from the stairs, my hands each had a mysterious object in them. The two objects look like compasses, but every three days, the needles move. I am sure that they point to the descending staircase. I am leaving now. This is my final entry. My journal and one of the compasses will stay with the remains of my camp. Goodbye."

Ethan flipped through the remaining pages of the journal, but all of them were blank. He really did go to the descending staircase. Just before Ethan closed the journal, a yellowed scrap of newspaper fell out of the back cover. He picked it up and read the headline *Frontier Town Hit with Phantom Plague: 341 killed.* It was dated for February of 1850.

"We need to find that compass before something horrible happens," Mason said with a blank face.

No one spoke. Ethan was shocked. He guessed that the stairs were evil, but nothing like this. It didn't seem real. "Can we be sure that this journal is telling the truth?" Ethan asked in desperation. He didn't want the responsibility. He didn't want it to be real. He wished that he never went looking for the stairs. And it still begged the question, why hadn't the Forest Service done anything about the problem? They must know that something bad was on the way.

"Come on Ethan," Alex said, "if they were hiding it in a secret safe, with decoys all around, they know that the journal is telling the truth. There's no way around it."

"Well, do you think the compass is—"

The window behind them shattered. Glass shards tinkled through the room, and a split second after the impact a gunshot cracked through the peaceful forest air.

"Get away from the window! We're being shot at," Mason screamed.

Ethan dove to the floor, scraping his elbows in broken glass. He scrambled backwards and braced himself against the wall. It shuddered as another round ripped through it. Ethan looked up to see a cloud of drywall powder billowing out of a bullet-sized hole in the wall. It was an exit wound, so Ethan couldn't be sure on the caliber, but it sounded like a rifle round. Not to mention that—crack—the sound of the shot came well after the impact.

"What do we do now?" Alex yelled from somewhere across the room. The shooting didn't stop. Three more rounds busted through the wall in quick succession. Semiautomatic.

Then the shooting paused. Ethan army-crawled through the glass on the hardwood floor to the base of the window. He huddled just below the sill, out of sight. "I'm going to peek up and try to see where it's coming from!"

"No, Ethan! That's dumb," Mason called, "If that's semiautomatic like I think it is, the barrel will likely be equipped with a flash hider! And even if it isn't, you probably couldn't see it anyway. Look through the bullet holes!"

He withdrew from the window, and instead peered through the bullet hole on the wall. It was about shoulder high. Just as Ethan's eyes started to adjust to looking through the hole, four more rounds ripped through the walls, and they were followed by the staccato, bang-bang-bang-bang, coming from the distance. Ethan gasped and ducked.

It must be the other forest rangers shooting at us. They're the only ones who know the importance of this place, Ethan thought. "It's the other rangers!" Ethan shouted to the room, "we need to confront them and get that compass!"

"We're pinned down!" Mason responded, "how do we get to them?"

"All of the shots are hitting this wall, which means they don't have a view of the front of the house," Alex said, "we can get to the truck."

"Yeah," Ethan continued, "and that means the shots are coming from the mountain behind the station. Mason!"

"What?"

"Is there a road to that mountain?" Ethan asked, gesturing at the window.

"Yeah, I think so. It doesn't matter, they'll shoot us on sight."

"No, they won't, I have a plan, but you'll have to trust me. Are you guys ready?"

"Yes."

"Sure."

"Okay," Ethan said, "on my mark, make a run for the truck. Alex, you're driving. Take us up to the top of that mountain. Mason, you give him directions. Ready? Now!"

They sprinted out from the living room and to the truck out front. The rangers must have seen movement through the windows because a handful of shots were fired, but none of them struck anywhere near the men. Ethan leaped into the back seat of the truck next to Mason. Alex slid into the driver's seat. "Pass me the keys," he ordered. Mason plunged his arm into his pocket and tossed them over the seat into Alex's hands.

He started the engine and tore out of the driveway. Ethan smelled burnt rubber.

"Turn right, here!" Mason ordered, arm stretched over the center console and his finger stabbing the air. Not slowing down, Alex wildly spun the wheel, throwing Mason into Ethan's lap with the force of the turn. This was why they never let Alex drive, normally.

Then he heard only the sound of a roaring engine. Ethan couldn't see the speedometer, but Alex had to be cruising at more than 95 miles per hour down the highway. The acceleration didn't stop. It was a good thing too, as a hail of bullets smashed into the ground near the truck. One bulled smashed through the windshield and put a hole in the center of the front passenger headrest. Ethan shuddered.

The bullets kept coming, and Alex had only covered half the distance to the base of the mountain. Ethan saw a flash of light at the top, and a split second later a bullet put a hole in the roof of the truck.

"Is everyone okay?" Alex called back.

Ethan responded, "I don't have any extra holes yet."

They reached the safety of the trees at the base of the mountain, and the rifle fire ceased. "Take this road, here," Mason said, pointing.

Alex pulled onto a sideroad that was almost as bad as the driveway to the fire lookout. It was full of switchbacks and washboards, and Alex had trouble making it up the road. He had to stop fully a few times, and nearly went careening into a ravine on one occasion. They continued, nonetheless.

Ethan drew the handgun that he took from mason and pulled the slide back a little to make sure a round was chambered. He released the slide and it snapped forward.

"What are you going to do with that thing," Mason asked with a hint of fear.

"Just act like you're afraid," Ethan said resolutely. He wanted to put off an aura of strength and confidence, but he wasn't sure his plan would work. "How close are we to the top?"

"I don't know," Mason said, "I've never been up here."

"What?" Alex yelled, "how the hell did you know where this road was?"

"Lucky guess… I guess."

Alex crested the hill. The road was flat from then on, with a thick canopy over the top and dense forest on either side. It was unnervingly dark. At the end of the road was a clearing, within which stood three figures. One stood at the front, holding a rifle, and the other stood with the third figure, holding a gun to his head. "Eric," Ethan whispered.

They slowed to a stop about twenty yards from the rangers. Before the leader had a chance to raise his rifle to the truck. Ethan kicked open his door and yanked Mason out with him, gripping firmly on his should. Mason tried to shake him off, "stop, that hurts."

"Shut up and play along," Ethan said coldly. He pushed Mason in front of him and put his handgun to his neck, making sure that it was visible to the leader. They walked forward.

"Wow, Mason," the leader said with mock laughter, "I can't believe that you were beaten by two restrained men. How pitiful."

Ethan saw Mason clench his fist. "Don't. Say. Anything." Ethan muttered through clenched teeth. He raised his voice to address the leader, "where's the compass that leads to the lair of Inferius?"

That seemed to set him off. His carefully crafted relaxed impression was tossed aside. "Asking questions about myths so soon? We haven't even introduced ourselves properly yet," he said in a calculated tone.

"You already know my name," Ethan said in a matching tone.

"But you don't know mine. I am District Ranger Williams. And this," he gestured at the man with the broken nose, "is one of my rangers."

"Okay then, Williams," Ethan spat, "Where's the compass at?"

"You just don't know when to stop, do you?" Williams growled. "I suggest we first discuss trading our hostages." Behind him, Ethan noticed that Eric was fidgeting next to his handler and glancing repeatedly at the two trucks parked in the clearing. Eric lost a hand to the stairs. That made him unpredictable. Ethan didn't like that.

"There's not much to discuss. You give me Eric, and I give you Mason."

"You first."

Ethan scowled. It would have to do. "Give 'em hell," he whispered to Mason, giving him a push. Mason crossed the divide between the two groups and stood next to Williams. No one moved.

"Send Eric over now."

"Ha, did you really think that would work? I already told you, you know too much. I can't have you or your friends causing trouble for my Forest Service," he gloated. Williams put his arm on Mason's shoulder.

The situation exploded. Mason threw a haymaker right into Williams' unsuspecting face, knocking him to the ground. The ranger with the broken nose reached for his holster, but Eric broke free from his grip. Eric then charged Williams, who had only just gotten back up, tackling him and finishing what Mason started. Williams' rifle clattered to the ground. Breaking free from his grapple with Williams in the dirt, Eric took it and threw it into the thick forest, out of sight. Then he ran for the trucks, a key ring jingling in his hand.

"Mason! Get in the truck!" Ethan shouted. He ran back, climbing into the driver's seat. Alex hopped in shotgun. By the time Mason clambered into the back, Eric drove right past them, kicking up dirt and rocks into the side of Mason's truck. Ethan slammed on the gas and shot into the clearing, using it as a turnaround. Someone fired a handgun.

Ethan finished the turn and accelerated back onto the road, following Eric's dust cloud. They raced down the road, ignoring any concern for safety. "He's going to climb the stairs!" Ethan shouted, pressing even harder on the gas pedal. Still, Eric kept gaining on them.

Driving like a madman, Ethan slammed his fists into the dashboard. They were so close! Why did Eric have to do this now? If they had stayed, maybe he could have pried the location of the compass out of Williams, but now Williams knew to hide it from them.

"After we find Eric," Alex said, "we need to get back to Williams to get the compass."

Ethan cursed. "No, we just took his leverage. He won't confront us directly without a meat shield to stop us from hurting him. And now he knows what we want: the compass."

"He knows the forest better than any of us," Mason said fearfully, "he can hide and wait us out."

This conversation was nothing more than a distraction. Ethan turned his attention back to the road. Eric was completely out of view, and Ethan was losing his trail. It didn't matter, he knew where he was going. Ethan pulled off Eric's path.

"Where are you going," Alex demanded.

"I'm taking a detour; we're going to cut him off." The truck's tires growled as they raced over the pavement, then roared when Ethan refused to slow down as the road turned to gravel again. He sped through the forest. Tree branches and low-hanging moss smacked into the truck. Ethan's stomach growled. *Well,* he thought, *I guess I haven't eaten since lunch yesterday.*

The detour didn't work; when they pulled into the secret pullout, Eric's stolen truck was already parked.

Alex slid out of Mason's truck and ran towards Eric's vehicle. Resting his hand on the hood, he announced, "he isn't far! The engine's still hot!"

They left the truck and crashed through the brush at a breakneck pace. Ethan gritted his teeth and picked up the pace, leaving his friends in the dust. He couldn't bear to lose Eric, and he couldn't bear to give any more power to that thing. Seven miles of wilderness sprinted past Ethan.

It was too much.

When he was almost at the stairs, Ethan began noticing signs of Eric. Broken twigs and swept-back ferns. He had to go faster. It didn't matter though.

Ethan barreled into the clearing. To nothing. Eric was not there. He stood unmoving, staring blank faced at the stairs. He fell to his knees.

About ten minutes later, Alex and Mason arrived, panting and out of breath. Alex looked around and said, "he's not here! We beat him!"

"No," Mason said to Alex under his breath.

And the smile drained from Alex's face. He approached Ethan, saying, "maybe—"

"Shut up."

"Ethan," Mason said, "we know that it's going to feed on Eric, but maybe he isn't dead yet. If we find the compass in time, we could save him."

Ethan inhaled, then breathed out shakily. Close to losing control, he pinched his thumb. "Okay," he said, "where do we start."

Chapter 11

Sitting in the back of the truck, Ethan spooned canned soup into his mouth. It was cold and gross, but it was all they had at the little store on the highway. He wished that he could go home and dig through his pantry to cook up a grand feast but going home now was not an option. Williams' goons knew where he lived, and they would surely be watching the house.

"This isn't working," Ethan said. He spat out a chunk of grisly meat.

"What," Mason asked over his can of pork and beans.

"The search, we're doing something wrong."

"We've only been searching for a few days. This forest is massive, and there are many Forest Service properties scattered through it. Williams could be at any one of them."

Ethan looked down, "the worst part is that we have to avoid being seen." Ethan lamented each day that passed. It was one more day that Eric spent in torment, dark and alone. "Why don't we just go directly to Williams' house?"

"I don't know what to tell you, Williams is a very private person, and I've been cut off from all my connections in the Forest Service. They don't trust me anymore. Besides, no one in the service knows where his secret cabin is."

"He has a secret cabin? Why didn't you tell us sooner?"

"I didn't think it would matter, it's impossible to find."

"That has to be where the compass is," Alex said.

Ethan frowned. "The Forest Service doesn't have any censorship powers, does it?"

"No," Mason said, confused, "what are you getting at?"

"Williams can't stop satellites from mapping his cabin. Our problem is that there are countless other cabins being mapped too. Lucky for us, we can access public records on our phones."

"That's a good idea!" Alex exclaimed, pulling out his phone at the same time as Ethan. They both navigated to the digital maps on their phones. "Mason, you too. Mark any cabins or remote buildings on your map that are in our area."

Ethan scrolled through the maps on his phone with renewed vigor. He was glad to finally have something tangible to do that would increase their chances of finding Williams and going down to save Eric from Inferius.

Mason and Alex, however, didn't seem so eager. While searching through miles of digital maps, Ethan watched as they both nodded off then woke back up every few seconds. They were exhausted. Alex's lack of dedication perturbed Ethan, but he couldn't really blame Mason, who didn't even know Eric.

In fact, Ethan realized, Mason had already done a great service just by sparing Ethan's life. That took balls, and now Mason was a jobless outlaw. *He really does care about serving and redeeming the Forest Service.*

Under the stars, Ethan sat in the bed of the truck and forewent sleep. By the time that the digital search was complete, the sun was nearly up. It didn't satisfy Ethan, though. Even if he worked all hours of the day and night, he wasn't working hard enough. He didn't know how much time Eric had, and every wasted second could be the second that could have saved his life if Ethan was just a little bit quicker. Only when this was all over would he rest. He would go home and sleep for a week.

Ethan concerned himself with the matter of confronting Williams. If it came down to it, Ethan wondered, looking at the pistol tucked in his belt, could he kill him? For the sake of everyone that could be affected by the disasters to come? Or simply to defend himself? It would be better to convince Williams to join them. But if he was so afraid of confronting the creature behind the stairs that he would try to murder innocent people to keep it a secret, what would it take to change his mind?

There's no good solution to this.

| | |

Early in the morning, after Alex and Mason had the chance to sleep, they combined their lists. Alex grabbed the addresses off all of them and started cross referencing them with public records.

"How do you know he didn't register his cabin with a secret name?" Mason asked.

Ethan replied, "he wouldn't have done that, the risk of being caught for fraud is too high. We're looking for a cabin that isn't in any of the records. And I suppose it is possible that all his paperwork is legit. In that case, we'll find his name in the records, then pay him a visit."

Mason looked down and put his hand on his knee to stop it from bouncing. He looked troubled and nervous. "Are you going to kill him?"

Ethan's face softened. "I hope not, but it might come to that. I thought you didn't like him, anyway."

"He has his flaws, and in hindsight I realize now that he's handled the situation with the stairs like a coward, but he was good to us. Harsh, but good. Leadership like his is what drives the good parts of the Forest Service."

"Then I will do my best to keep the peace, but if he continues to prevent us from doing what needs to be done…" Ethan let the implication hang in the air.

"I understand."

Ethan put his hand on Mason's shoulder, and they sat on the side of the truck, gazing out to the forest.

"Holy shit!" Alex exclaimed from behind them. Ethan scowled at the interruption.

"What is it?" Mason demanded, turning around to go to Alex.

"There haven't been any off the grid cabins yet, but I just found one that has the deed in the name of one Mary Williams."

"Does he have a wife?" Ethan asked of Mason.

"Not that I know of. Maybe it's his mother, or a cousin."

"There isn't much information here," Alex said, "it might just be a coincidence.

Ethan looked over Alex's shoulder at the address listed on the record. "It's not far from here," he said, "we can show up and ask, and if he's not there, we won't have wasted too much time."

"Mount up," Mason called, hopping behind the wheel.

| | |

For a secret cabin, it looked quite homely. Flowerbeds circled its small base, and hanging pots decorated the porch. The grass was nicely kept and the pink paint fresh.

It sat alone at the crest of a hill. It was invisible from the road below, and the driveway was marked with ominous signs that declared, *Private Driveway*, and, *Do Not Enter*. They ignored the warnings, the possibility of getting shot at was there regardless of whether this was Williams' cabin or not.

"This doesn't seem like Williams," Mason whispered in front of the house.

"Let's just knock and find out," Ethan replied with a similarly hushed tone. He approached the door. *Here goes nothing*, he thought while double checking that his handgun was easy to reach. He rapped the door twice with his knuckles.

From inside, he heard a television go mute, and then slow, deliberate footsteps approaching the door. They stopped before the door, and Ethan reflexively reached behind him, ready to draw at a moment's notice.

Two deadbolts unlocked, and the door swung inward. A short old woman stood before Ethan. "Hello," she smiled, "what can I do for you?"

Ethan peered inside, looking for a sign of Williams, but he saw nothing. "Do you have any relation to District Ranger William?" he said with the politest voice he could muster.

"Oh, John?" she said, "of course! He's my grandson! Are you boys some of his friends?"

"Umm, yeah," Ethan said uneasily.

"Oh, that's just wonderful, he's never brought visitors of his own up here before! It's too bad though, he won't be back for another hour or two. Some errand for the Forest Service. He's the District Ranger, you know? Come inside," she gestured, "have something to eat and drink while we wait for him!"

Ethan glanced back at Alex and Mason. They shrugged, as if to say, *it's up to you*. Something to eat. That sounded good. "Of course," he said, smiling, "thanks for the hospitality."

She led them inside to a small living room. "Now, you boys just wait right here," she said pointing to a sofa, "I will be right back with some snacks."

Ethan gratefully sat on the couch. It looked like it was fifty years old, with floral print, but it was in pristine condition. He looked around the room, searching for clues about Williams, or John, as he now knew, but it looked like a normal house.

Williams' grandmother returned shortly with a plate piled high with pastries. Ethan hungrily accepted it, and she sat in an armchair diagonal to the couch. "So, is it just the two of you up here?" Mason asked.

"Yes," she said, "ever since John was a young boy, he told me that he would get me a cabin in the woods, and he would be there to take care of me. When he was younger, I just assumed that he had an overactive imagination, but he kept his promise, and here we are."

"What does he like to do on his downtime here? we don't see him much outside of work."

She chuckled, "I'm afraid his work seems to follow him home. He's always obsessing about something or other that relates to the Forest Service. He does have one hobby, however. His room is filled with antiques that he's collected over the years, relics from even before my time."

Ethan's eyes widened. "Do you think we could see his collection?"

"Oh, I don't know," she worried, "he doesn't even like it when I look at his artifacts, you'll have to ask him when he gets back."

Ethan disguised his frustration, willing to wait. He didn't want to pull this innocent woman into their conflict. "How long have you two lived up here?"

"About fifteen years," she said, "right after he got a job with the Forest Service. I made the down payment, and the house is in my name, but he's made all of the mortgage payments since then."

"What was he like back then? When he first joined?" Mason asked.

"He was incredibly optimistic; he loved his job. Every day he came home and told me about a project he was working on or something he did that day to help people." Her expression darkened, "but over the years, as he got promotion after promotion, the optimism has gone away. I know that the happy young man he used to be is still there, but something is troubling him. He won't talk about it, but I think he's afraid of something. It makes him ashamed, I believe."

Ethan looked at Mason and saw a glimmer of hope in his eyes. If they could just get Williams on their side…

A car door slammed out front.

"That must be my grandson!" she exclaimed, "wait here and I will go get him." She hobbled out of the room and into the hallway. Ethan heard her open the door and shout, "John! Some of your friends have come to visit!"

But he already knew that. He had to, given that their truck was parked right in front of the cabin. Williams stormed into the living room; his face painted with rage. But then he looked back at his grandmother, and when he fixed his gaze on Ethan and his friends again, it was one of fear.

Doing his best to fake a smile and a cheery attitude, Ethan said, "John! Let's go outside, we need to talk about something from work."

Shaking with fear, he obliged the request, and the four men left the cabin. Ethan leaned against Mason's truck, casually drawing a circle in the dirt with his foot. "I'm going to assume that you have the compass in your room."

Williams may have been violent, vindictive, and even cowardly, but he wasn't stupid. He was outnumbered and, if it came to it, he could not defend himself or his grandmother. Ethan would never hurt her, or even involve her of course, but Williams didn't know that. Ethan wasn't inclined to correct his ignorance, either.

He nodded, "yes, I have it here."

"Go get it for me." Williams turned to leave, but Ethan stopped him. "Give me your rifle before you go in there."

A look of betrayal clouded Williams' expression, but he complied, grabbing it from the back seat of his truck. He handed it to Ethan, who examined it closely. *An AR-10*, Ethan recognized, *at least he's a man with a good taste for rifles*. Ethan pulled back the charging handle, chambering a round.

After disappearing into the cabin for a few minutes, Williams returned with an ornate compass, and placed it into Ethan's outstretched palm. Giving it up caused Williams to grimace in pain. *The compass must mean something to him*, Ethan thought with a hint of remorse.

As for the compass, it was beautiful. The needle was made of polished silver, trapped beneath glass that was set into a beautiful dark wood. Swirling carvings lined with gold leaf wrapped around the compass. They made Ethan think of the number six.

"The needle points in a new direction every three days at noon, but you already know that." Williams checked his watch and continued, "that should be in about ten minutes."

"John, why won't you face the stairs? Is it because the higher ups won't let you?"

"I—" Williams looked down at his feet, ashamed and unable to answer.

"You are brave enough to go on a crusade against any who might alert the public, but you can't face the real problem. If we don't make it out of the descending staircase alive, then I expect you to continue our fight," Ethan said. He shoved William's rifle back into his arms, then climbed into the truck with Alex and Mason. As they left the property, Ethan peeked back one more time, and saw that Williams was still looking at his feet. He thought he saw a single tear roll down his cheek.

Chapter 12

Like clockwork, the needle of the compass shifted at noon. Now it pointed west. "What's the plan?" Alex asked, "we know where Eric is, but how are we going to fight the demon that is at the bottom of the descending staircase?"

"The deadline to kill the thing is much farther out than the deadline to save Eric, so let's focus on one thing it a time," Ethan explained, "I say we just pop down there, grab Eric, and get out. We can worry about doing the Forest Service's job for them later." He looked at Mason. "No offense."

"None taken."

Following the direction of the compass was difficult. The roads rarely aligned with the needle of the compass, so most of the navigation was guesswork. Slowly, they narrowed down on the position of the descending staircase, until the roads could go no closer. Mason parked his truck in a clearing off to the side of a gravel road, and the trio disembarked. Ethan used the compass to lead them, walking through the wilderness like they did before.

They thrashed their way through thick underbrush. "I wonder what this reminds me of," Ethan commented sarcastically. The dry humor helped Ethan to mask his fear. He was terrified of what he would find down there. He was terrified that he might perish. He feared that he would be inadequate to face the evil at the heart of the stairs, but most of all, he was afraid that he was too late. It was a very real possibility that Eric was already dead, especially if there was no water at the bottom of the descending staircase.

He pushed on, though. There was no other choice. Despite his fear, he would face his—and the world's—demons. That's the meaning of courage, isn't it? He pushed Eric into this mess by taking him on a misguided quest, so he would get him out.

The compass began to vibrate in Ethan's hand. He took it as a symbol that they were close. "Stay on your toes, guys," he said.

In the distance was a clearing, and its vibrant green light filtered in between the tree trunks of the forest. They quickened their pace, anxious to get to their destination. Ethan moved his handgun from behind his back to his front hoodie pocket, ensuring easy access. He hoped he would not need it, and not just because he didn't want a fight; a pistol probably wouldn't affect anything down there.

Ethan almost expected to see another monolithic staircase, but this was just a regular meadow. There was no sign of a descending staircase. Excitedly shaking in Ethan's hand, the compass said otherwise. Ethan walked in a circle around the meadow to get a better reading of direction, and the needle consistently pointed at a rock face about fifty yards away from the meadow. When he first entered the clearing, the face seemed unimportant, but under closer scrutiny, he saw a man-sized opening near the base. A deep, red glow emanated from the passage.

Pointing at the rock face, Ethan said, "there it is. Let's go get our friend."

Up close, the stone wall was a climber's dream. Not even a single patch of moss grew on the rocks, and countless crevices, ledges, and holes turned the rock face into a staircase for anyone that knew what to look for. Too bad Ethan didn't need to go up anymore.

He turned his attention to the cavity. Alex and Mason stood with him in the mouth of the cave—and up close he could tell that it was a cave—staring into its depths. Ten feet in, it curved down and to the left, but he couldn't see anything other than that. Deep, red light pulsed from its belly, reflecting off the cold walls and the primitive steps cut into the stone floor. This staircase was ancient.

And they hesitated. They had no idea what they were going up against, and they had no idea how to find Eric down there. So much could go wrong.

Ethan pushed forward and stepped into the mouth of the cave. Shards of rock jutted from the top of the opening. They reminded him of teeth. He stopped, just one step in. Silence.

Even though he was just a score of inches inside the cave, the ambient noise of the forest never reached his ears. His friends' inquisitive voices were muffled and distant. Somewhere down the stone cut staircase, a stream of water trickled. Wind blew up from the depths, as if the cave were breathing. And the red glow still illuminated the cave. Only when it was taken away from him did Ethan realize how much he needed to hear natural noise. Sound was particularly important to the stairs, it seemed that they used it to signify the difference between reality and the twisted patches of darkness that they created.

Ethan shuddered and stepped back out of the cave. It was like coming to the surface of a lake. Rustling leaves and singing birds reminded Ethan that he was still safe. Turning to advise his friends on the situation, he saw that their attention was occupied elsewhere.

They glared towards the meadow, at an approaching figure. Williams. *Shit*, Ethan thought, pulling his handgun.

"What do we do now?" Alex asked, "I won't let him stop us, not this close."

"Don't do anything yet," Mason said, "he's got his rifle, so he outranges us."

Ethan held his gun at a low ready, hoping again that he wouldn't need to use it. Worried he may have been, but panic had yet to manifest. Williams had his rifle slung on his back, so Ethan would have at least some advance warning before being fired upon. They stood and waited as Williams approached.

As he got closer, and his face became clear, and something about his downcast expression caught Ethan off guard. Was that… remorse? Williams refused to make eye contact with the men as he approached. Then when he arrived, he stood before Ethan, fear and determination in his eyes.

"I thought about what you said to me. I'm done hiding from this. Fuck whatever my higher ups have to say."

Shocked, Ethan tilted his head and shook his hand. He clapped Williams on the shoulder. "What changed your mind?"

Shrugging, Williams explained, "I realized what I was doing to you guys. What I was willing to do the keep the stairs a secret, and how I was doing it at the expense of the community that I'm supposed to serve. I realized the error in my ways."

"So, you're here to help us rescue Eric?"

"I'm here to kill the beast that's causing all of this." Williams drew an ornate, ceremonial-looking dagger. Red lines ran up and down in swirling patterns on the polished blade. Strips of leather encircled the handle, and unrecognizable symbols were embossed along the entire weapon. "At Some point in the past century, this relic was created to put an end to the horrors caused by the stairs. It was never used."

"How does it work?"

"I don't know, when I discovered it in my younger days, I was searching for information about the stairs that my superiors refused to give me. Only years later did I finally discover what it was for."

Ethan raised an eyebrow. "Do you really think that's going to work?"

Sighing, Williams said, "I do not know, but I must try. This is my redemption. If Inferius is slain by my hand, I will be poised to take control of the Forest Service and turn it away from its cowardly ways. And if I fail? Well, if I die down there, then none of this will be my problem anymore."

"Wait, you can just take over the Forest Service if you kill this thing." Ethan was pleased with Williams' change of heart, but his motivation made Ethan uneasy.

"Ethan, you walked into this conflict just a few weeks ago, but I have lived it my entire adult life. There is much you do not understand. If we make it out of that cave, maybe you can join me."

"Don't count on it," Ethan said with light sardonicism.

"Wait, how did you follow us here?" Alex asked.

"Didn't you read the journal? Two compasses were created, and I managed to recover both."

"Okay, we need to worry about all these pleasantries later," Mason finally said, giving an extra glare to Williams. It seemed like he was jealous. Or angry. "What's the plan to kill this thing and rescue Eric?"

Ethan said, "Williams has the best gun here, and the dagger, so he can split up from us to distract and fight Inferius while Mason, Alex, and I search for Eric."

"That sounds good," Alex said. He had his chest puffed out, trying to convince himself that he wasn't afraid. Ethan couldn't judge him; he felt the same way.

"No, I want to go with Williams," Mason argued, "we've worked together before and, no offense, Ethan, but Eric is your friend, not mine. Inferius has plagued the Forest Service since its inception. I want my pound of flesh."

"It's settled then," Ethan said. "Good luck everyone, we'll need it."

Chapter 13

Ethan took the first step. Again, all sound from outside the cave was either silenced or muffled. If he closed his eyes, it sounded like he was hundreds of feet underground, even though daylight was just a few steps away. The cave smelled of blood.

The stuffy air made Ethan cringe. He pushed on though, leading his group deeper into the cave. Soon enough, the vibrant sunlight was gone, replaced by the pulsing, red glow. Ethan pulled his phone from his pocket to use its flashlight, but it refused to turn on at all. "What the…" he whispered. Turning around, he realized that the same problem plagued his friends as well.

Deeper down, the humidity grew to unbearable levels, and the stone staircase grew slippery. A waft of steamy, warm air slammed into Ethan. This was no normal cave. He cursed and nearly vomited. He wished he could turn back, but Eric needed him.

Ethan took notice of the cave ceiling. It was laced with lumpy, red tubes snaking their way across, down the walls, and into crevices and cracks. He pointed them out to his friends, realizing that they were the source of the light. Looking to Alex for advice, Ethan pulled his pocketknife and gestured at one of the low hanging tendrils. Alex simply shrugged.

Ethan stabbed the tentacle with the tip of his knife, and it squirted putrid black liquid all down his arm. Somewhere in the distance he thought he heard a faint growl, and the odor of blood intensified. Williams coughed.

I've been away from home for over a week, sleeping in the bed of a truck that isn't mine, and now I'm climbing down into a paranormal cave to fight a demon that has no known weaknesses, all because another man wasn't willing to face his own responsibilities. And now, the same man who shot at me from a mountaintop, is standing behind me, better armed than I am.

He wanted to turn around and scream at Williams. But that wouldn't help. *Williams is here to help*, he told himself. Fighting with his allies would only help Inferius and the stairs, so he stayed quiet.

The unbearable, stuffy air did have the advantage of giving Ethan enough lethargy that he didn't feel the need to have an emotional outburst. He continued walking down the stairs in silence; there was nothing of importance to say.

After what felt like an eternity of walking, the stairs transitioned into an uneven, cramped hallway. The putrid tubes—Ethan assumed that they were analogous to blood vessels—covered the walls and floor now. Because of them, the ground wasn't level, and the height of the ceiling fluctuated. In some parts Ethan could stand on the tips of his toes, and in others he had to crawl. In the rare parts of the floor that weren't covered in veins, the black fluid pooled. It was light and slippery, and it smelled faintly of dirty motor oil.

Ethan almost missed it. On his right, the veins curved into a hole just big enough for a man to crawl through. He poked his head into it but could neither hear nor see anything.

"We're not here to explore," Williams exclaimed, "let's keep moving."

Ethan's pulled his lip back into a snarl. Was Williams really trying to tell him what to do? "Maybe you aren't, but I have a friend to save, and he could be in any one of these nooks. Don't try to tell me how to do this, if you hadn't pulled him back into this whole mess he would still be sitting at home in his apartment."

Williams said nothing more after that. Ethan surprised himself with the outburst. Just moments ago, he was trying to avoid such a tantrum. Maybe it was the cave, or the stress, or something much more sinister, but he was getting terribly irritable.

He wriggled through the hole and popped out onto the other side. The ceiling wasn't too short, but if he wanted to stand, he still had to bend his head forward to avoid rubbing against the putrid tubes.

The light was even lower in this room, so Ethan took a few short—something crunched under his foot. He reached down to pick it up and returned with a shard of a white solid. Ceramic?

Ethan searched the room, his eyes more adjusted to the minimal light, and then he saw them. Thousands of skulls. Some were stacked in neat piles, while many littered the floor, like the one he stepped on.

He yelped and scrambled back through the hole. As his foot left the evil room, he thought he felt something brush his calf, but was almost certain he imagined it.

Fifty yards further down the hallway there was a split. Five different hallways went in different directions. Thanks to the low light, it was impossible to see what was at the ends. "How do we know which way to go?" Alex asked.

"It's a maze, we're not supposed to know where to go. It wants us to wander and get lost."

Until now, there was only one hallway, but with the fork arose a new concern. "How will we know the way back up if we wander aimlessly," Ethan asked.

"Ethan," Williams said evenly, "I think this just went from a rescue mission to a kill mission. If we don't take out Inferius, we'll never escape. If we do defeat him…"

"Then we'll have enough time to wander in search of the exit," Ethan finished. He clicked his tongue, "what a terrible situation."

"Like that's new," Williams laughed, without a smile.

Down the middle hallway came a groan. It was barely audible, but unmistakably human. Reinvigorated, Ethan hissed, "Eric's this way," before dashing down the tunnel. He thought he heard either Williams or Mason protesting his dash, but Alex followed close behind him. They splashed through the black liquid on the floor and trampled the veiny tubes.

The groans grew in volume, and it became clear that they were from Eric; Ethan recognized his voice. He couldn't have been more than a hundred yards away, accounting for how far his voice could echo through the sinister cave.

In the dim light, the end of the hallway ended abruptly, and the red vascular walls flowed into a natural stone cave. Water trickled out of a hole near the roof of the cave and flowed into a pool. Sitting on the edge of the pool was Eric, covered in dirt. His hair was filthy, and he bore a gaunt expression.

"Eric! We're here to get you out!" Ethan screamed.

The announcement had little effect on Eric. He looked up at Ethan, but instead of jumping in elation, a mask of suspicion creeped over his face. His eyes narrowed and he tilted his head.

Just before Ethan reached Eric's cave, the red veins contracted from every direction to seal off the end of the hallway. They writhed like a bucket of squirming maggots to seal off every crack that led to the cave. In motion, they sounded like swirling macaroni and cheese, squelching and squeezing past each other. At the end of their reformation they hardened into an impenetrable wall, as strong as steel.

Still running at full speed, Ethan smashed into the wall, but it would not budge. He beat at the wall with his fists. Pulling his pocketknife, Ethan raked the honed blade across the wall. All that he got as a result was a shower of black blood.

Ethan halfheartedly slammed his shoulder into the wall. He was so close. Eric was right there, and it was still a straight shot back to the surface, too! He slumped to the floor as the others caught up with him.

And he couldn't even imagine what Eric was feeling now. After being trapped in a demon's cave for days without food or hope, he finally saw Ethan coming to rescue him. He seemed suspicious, the sensory deprivation likely made him question his own senses, but some part of him must have been glad to see Ethan there to rescue him. And then that hope was ripped away without warning.

Ethan imagined Eric sitting in that dark cave, convincing himself that it wasn't really Ethan. That it was his mind playing tricks, or it was some cruel torment. Either way, his hope was surely gone now.

"Get up, Ethan, we need to keep moving," Williams commanded pulling Ethan to his feet. To their left, a new passage was open.

"He's herding us right where he wants us to go," Alex observed.

"I know," Williams admitted, "but we have no choice but to face Inferius. He obviously won't let you get to Eric yet. Let's stick together and get him after we kill Inferius."

Ethan shook his head and frowned, following Williams down the new path. Just like that, his control of the situation was gone, and like Eric, he was left hopeless. The red light dimmed for a split second, and Ethan thought he saw movement up ahead. "Did you…"

"I saw it too," Mason said.

Williams raised his rifle, ready to fire. They saw nothing more for ten minutes, but after rounding a bend and entering a cavernous, vein-covered room, he was there. Inferius stood on a raised patch of red matter in the center of the room. It appeared to be an altar.

At least eight feet tall, the beast stood on spindly legs and had sticks for arms. Its skin looked like old leather. Yellow lichen clung to half of its body. There was an extra joint in its legs, just below the knee, that bent backwards, giving the demon the appearance of a grasshopper that was poised to leap forward.

Inferius rubbed his claw-like fingers together as if he were a scheming villain. His face was the worst part. Glowing, green orbs sat recessed in his façade, staring with pure hate, and right below them was a cavernous maw with endless rows of teeth. His ears were pointed triangles that stuck out to the side of his head.

Without thinking, Ethan fired four rounds from his handgun at the demon, and Williams fired double that with his rifle. Every single round struck its target, but none had any effect on Inferius, who leaped upward into a hole in the ceiling, right above the alter, that Ethan failed to notice before.

"That thing just ate a dozen rounds!" Ethan shouted in disbelief.

"Stay calm, we still have the dagger," Williams said. Ethan could tell that Williams' calm façade was wavering. The ranger stalked over to that altar and hopped up top, looking at the hole above him. A handful of the veins hung down from the rim of the passage in the ceiling, and Williams grabbed them, preparing to climb up.

Mason hopped onto the alter and prepared to do the same.

"Guys, wait," Alex commanded, "this is an altar room, and you aren't even going to look? There could be something here to help us."

"You guys look around down here," Mason said, "I'll scout up top." He scurried up the vein, climbing it like a rope, then disappeared over the edge on top.

Williams was more thoughtful. He joined Ethan and Alex in their investigation of the altar room. Around the edge of the room were corpses. Not nearly as many as in the room with the old bones that Ethan found before, but there were a few dozen.

Some were older than others. One dead man looked as if he had been dead for less than a month, with flesh still hanging on his rotting body, while many of the corpses were just skeletons that still had their clothes. Strangely, though, the bodies were odorless.

On the opposite side of the room, Williams approached one that had an outfit straight out of the fifties. He reached into the dead man's pocket and took a notebook. Ethan caught a glimpse of the cover; it read, *Field Notes*.

There wasn't much else in the room. One by one, they climbed the veins that drooped from the opening above. Unsurprisingly, it opened into a hallway not much different from the others.

"Wait, where the hell did Mason go?" Alex asked, trying his best to peer down the hallway through the gloom.

Williams' eyes widened, and he began frantically searching all his pockets and the small bag he had on his back. "That little shit stole the dagger!"

"What?" Ethan was shocked. Mason was as dedicated to saving Eric and killing Inferius as he was. "Why would he do that, is he trying to get back out of here and leave us?"

"No," Williams growled, seething with cold rage, "he's going to kill the beast to take all the glory for himself."

Ethan couldn't believe what he was hearing. "This isn't about glory! We're here to rescue Eric and kill this thing, not claim glory."

"Tell that to Mason," Williams growled.

"What are you going to gain from this glory, though? We can't go public with any of this."

"Not public glory, but within the Forest Service. Inferius is our greatest enemy, and whoever slays him will demand respect from every member of the organization. I will do good with that power; can you say the same about Mason?"

Ethan didn't like that Williams was trying to split the group, but maybe he was right. He kept his mouth shut, not wanting to provoke Williams. They pushed onward, regardless of it was a trap or not.

A roar came from the distance. It was loud and deep, but it was accompanied by a high-pitched shriek that wrapped around the bass of the call. Ethan clapped his hands over his ears to block out the noise, and the red glow coming from the vascular walls went dark. They were blind.

"He's killing it now!" Williams barked. His footsteps echoed and splashed down the hallway.

"Williams! Stop!" Ethan shouted. There was no reply. Within seconds, the light returned, and the direction that they came from was blocked off. Instead, a new passaged curved to the right. "Dammit! They're falling for its tricks." Ethan turned to Alex, "isn't it obvious that it's trying to split us up!"

Alex nodded in horror.

Ethan gripped his pistol even tighter than before. He only had eleven rounds left. It wasn't like that would make a difference, though, the first four hurt the demon about as much as a foam dart would hurt a man.

He thought he heard gunshots in the distance.

This new tunnel was not nearly as straight as the other ones. It curved up and down, and it snaked in every direction. At some points, Ethan thought he was going in circles. "It's stalling us," Ethan said.

"Well, there's nothing we can do about it now, just remember to think carefully at the next crossroads, we need to stick together and reunite with the rangers."

The hallway ended with a hole in the floor like its start. But this time the hole dropped down to Eric's cave! Ethan hungrily grabbed a vein and slid down to the floor of the cave. On the way down, it dawned on him that it was a bit of a hasty decision—he was being led to Eric for a reason—but he couldn't help himself.

Ethan ran to Eric and tackled him in a hug, while Eric laid like a dead fish on the ground for a moment, but he soon rebounded and embraced Ethan with more intensity than the tackle. "You're real!" Eric said with a raspy voice.

"Of course, I'm real, we're going to get you out of here."

Breathing heavy, Eric rambled, "they've tormented me with visions and voices, but none of them ever touched me."

"Wait, what do you mean by 'they'?"

"The demons that are down here," Eric shuddered.

"Ethan, we don't have time to debrief, get him up and let's go," Alex said.

Nodding, Ethan pulled Eric to his feet, and the three started walking towards the hallway that they first saw Eric through—it was no longer blocked.

A gunshot roared through the cave behind them. Ethan whipped around to find the source of the blast but saw nothing. That is, until another burst of three rounds fired and he saw a faint muzzle flash come from a crevice just big enough for him to fit through.

"Alex, you know the way back from here, take Eric up. I can't just leave Mason and Williams to die." Alex started to protest, but Ethan was already running towards the back of the cave. He didn't look back.

It was a tight fit, and Ethan scraped his back on a shard of rock, but he popped through the other side to a cave about the same size as the previous one. Mason was on the ground with a pool of blood around his head, and Williams was on his back, kicking at Inferius. It loomed over him, swiping with its claws.

The dagger was on the ground next to Mason. Its blade was tarnished with foul black blood. Ethan aimed his handgun and put one round into the side of the creature's head. It snapped to the side, but the beast didn't crumple to the ground like a person would from a shot to the brain. Instead, Inferius turned to Ethan and gave him a bloodcurdling smile, baring its numerous teeth in an open-mouthed grin that stretched up to the corners of its eyes.

Ethan lunged for the dagger, kicking himself into the air. As he sailed past the demon, it swiped at him, clipping his right forearm. Three quarters of the way to the dagger, Ethan slammed into the stone floor and slid the rest of the way. He grabbed the now-slippery handle and swung around just in time to face the creature. It reared back, ready to strike him with a killing blow to the abdomen, but Ethan was faster. He swiped the dagger at the beast's ropey neck.

It made the same screech that he heard in the hallway earlier. Ethan squeezed his eyes shut. He felt like he was going deaf from the noise.

When he opened his eyes, the creature was gone. In its place was a puddle of the same black blood that decorated his blade. For a moment, Ethan was proud, but Williams spoke to change that. "Don't get your hopes up," he said, "it's not dead."

The red light went dark like before, then flickered back to life. "I cut its throat with the dagger, you said that it could kill it!"

"The dagger is more effective than bullets, but it seems that its creator did not make it strong enough."

Ethan weakly limped to Mason, who was still laying in his own blood. "What happened?" he asked Williams in shock.

"The beast threw him into the wall, I caught up with him here just after it happened."

For some reason, Ethan didn't trust that that was the full story, but it didn't matter now. "Come on, we need to get out of here. Alex and Eric are already on their way to the staircase, they might already be up. Help me carry Mason."

"Ethan," Williams said with disdain, "we've come all this way to just leave without killing Inferius?"

"Maybe you have, but I only came here to rescue my friend. The plan's changed, we're going to meet up with them and get out of here to fight another day."

Williams hesitated but acquiesced. "Fine, I'll leave with you, but I can no longer turn a blind eye to the tyranny of the stairs. And when I return, I want you by my side to help fight this thing. You're a part of this now, and I could use your help in the future."

Ethan wasn't sure how he felt about that.

Williams, being larger and stronger than Ethan, chose to carry Mason on his own. Ethan helped him get through the crevice to the cave with the lake, but from then on Williams alone bore Mason's weight. Ethan led the way back, entering the veiny tunnel. With Williams slowed by Mason, it seemed like they walked for miles before returning to the fork in the road.

Except it was no longer a fork. All the other passageways were closed, leaving the way back to the staircase as the only option. The hair on the back of Ethan's neck raised up. They were still pawns in the demon's game.

Ethan and Alex determined before that it was trying to split them up to control them, and they vowed to not be separated.

"Shit," Ethan whispered, that was exactly what they did when Ethan went to help Williams. It should have been obvious, why else would it have led them right to Eric, then fought Mason and Williams in the next cave over? "We have to go faster! Alex and Eric are in danger!"

"How do you know?"

"This thing's been playing with us since we got here, and I fell for it again!"

"Well, there isn't anything we can do about it now, let's just get out of here."

"I have a bad feeling that it's not going to be that easy."

Carrying Mason prevented Williams from going much faster than a light jog. Ethan cursed the length of the hallway, he needed to get to Alex and Eric.

Ethan detached. The cave around him seemed unreal. It was unreal. None of it should have been there. Yet, here he was, playing right into the hand of the demon at the center of it. Ethan closed his eyes, imagining that he was still at the opening of the cave. In the daydream, he turned and walked away, he walked away from the cave and all the trouble with the stairs. *I never should have gotten myself into this.*

He felt something shaking his shoulder. Opening his eyes, he was still in the cave. He wanted to scream. Williams shook his shoulder, "get up Ethan, we have to keep going."

"No," he said, hiding his face, "leave me here, I'm done fighting."

"That's not an option," Williams said. Ethan looked in his eyes and saw frustration, but there was also a great deal of empathy there. "I understand, but your friends need you. Leaders don't get to give up. You can stop fighting when we get out of here, and if we don't… well, you'll have an eternity to rest."

Ethan ground his teeth together. He knew that Williams was right. Taking his outstretched hand, Ethan allowed himself to be pulled to his feet. He started walking again.

"You know, Ethan, despite all the trouble you've caused me, I really admire you for pushing the issue of the stairs," Williams said. "You were doing what you knew was right for your community. You were doing my job when I was too afraid to do it. Your actions are why I chose to face this beast, and not continue running from it."

Ethan took a deep breath and centered himself. "Thank you, that really helps." He relaxed a bit, then remembered something. "Earlier, you said that you want you by my side in the future."

"Of course, the stairs aren't the only threat that the Forest Service deals with."

After being gone for so long, Ethan was quite sure that his boss wouldn't let him back to work without some questions, and besides, Ethan couldn't imagine going back to his old life. "If we make it out of here alive," he said, "I'm going to take you up on your offer, but on one condition: no more running. I will join so that we can face these things head on."

"That's exactly why I want you."

For a brief few moments, Ethan was put at ease. He was glad for the new opportunity, of course, but it was probably the act of talking about the future that convinced his fight-or-flight response that imminent death was no longer a threat.

All that came to an end.

Ethan and Williams arrived at the entrance to the cave. Eric and Alex were slouched against the walls on either side of the hallway. As they got closer, Ethan was able to see through the red haze behind them. The stairway was blocked off by a writhing mass of veins. The tubes surged past each other, reinforcing the barricade. Inferius really didn't want them to leave.

Taking short shallow breaths, Ethan approached Alex and Eric; they were obviously past the panic stage. "W-what happened," he stuttered.

"It closed off right as we got here," Eric croaked.

"I've tried to cut through it with my knife," Alex gestured at the barrier, "but it was no use."

Oozing black blood flowed from countless cuts to the veins, but it seemed unaffected. Alex had a splash of the fluid on his face, too. "I can tell," Ethan remarked.

"We need do decide on a plan of action," Williams said, laying Mason down.

"No, that's not possible. What I've learned from being down here for so long is that this demon will take its time with you and act on its own terms. All we can do is wait and maybe kill it by luck," Eric said nonchalantly.

"There's nothing we can do to prepare?"

"You could keep slashing at that barrier like a child throwing a tantrum," Eric said coldly.

Ethan looked at the dagger in his hand. They'd only tried cutting the veins with regular knives so far, and if the dagger was more effective on the beast, then maybe…

He lifted the dagger over his head and threw a cut with the force of his bodyweight behind it. It sliced clean through the barrier. Inferius screamed from not too far away, down the tunnel.

For a split second, the stairs were visible, and the gap was big enough that Ethan could have slipped through. He cheered. But as fast as he made the cut, twice as many veins grew in tightly to fill the gap.

Now he knew how Eric must have felt when he first called out to him. Hope given then ripped away.

Ethan threw three more sloppy cuts, opening a bigger hole which was filled back with more fervor than he made it with. The roars that came from these cuts were closer.

"Stop! It's not going to work!" Alex yelled, "you're just making it angrier!"

Mason sat up, groggily searching for the source of the yelling. Then he seemed to remember where he was and clambered to his feet. Looking around like a trapped animal, he exclaimed, "the dagger! I lost the dagger!"

"No," Ethan said, "I have it right here, I took it when you got knocked out."

"Oh," he said, confused, "then where are—"

A roar from only a handful of yards away interrupted Mason. At the same time, the vein walls of the tunnel started writhing with a horrible sucking and slurping noise, like a fat man eating spaghetti. The shadow of the beast was just barely visible down the tunnel.

The walls expanded, and their disgusting noises grew louder. When they were done, the reformed chamber was twice the size as the altar room from before. As a result of their transformation, the veins torrentially dripped the black flued down the walls. Luckily enough, none flowed from the ceiling, leaving the men dry. The stood on one side of the room, while Inferius stood on the other. Ethan drew his handgun and held it in his right hand with the dagger in his left.

Neither side moved.

Ethan whispered to Williams, "when I shot it in the head earlier, it seemed to take a bit more notice, maybe if I do the same with the dagger—"

Inferius shrieked and charged. Ethan and Williams emptied their guns at the thing. It didn't slow down. Ethan dropped his gun and tossed the dagger into his dominant hand, and just before the creature ripped him and Williams to pieces, he swiped it across the beast's chest. It shrieked again and stepped back, but it did not run.

It's done playing with us, Ethan realized, *this is it, time to fight or die.*

Ethan charged, shouting a war cry that scared himself more than anyone else. With a quick slash, he cut off two of the beast's fingers at the first knuckle. In response, it picked Ethan up like he was nothing, and threw him to the other side of the room. Ethan felt its putrid, scratchy flesh against his bare arms, and he shuddered. Its breath had the rancid, sweet scent of rotting meat mixed with the smell of vomit. Ethan avoided looking it in the eyes as it picked him up; he was afraid he would see something horrible in their depths.

At the end of his arc through the air, he slammed into the ground, nearly impaling himself with the holy dagger. In addition, he choked down a splash of the black fluid. It reminded him of the time when he accidentally swallowed some motor oil while emptying his truck's oil pan.

He hopped to his feet to face the beast, assuming it was coming to finish him off, but it was nowhere near him. Across the room, he watched in horror as it swiped a claw across Williams' face. A squirt of blood flowed down the ranger's cheek, and the low red light of the cave amplified the angry red cut that ran from just above his left eyebrow, all the way down to his jawline.

Yelling again, Ethan sprinted across the uneven footing, dagger outstretched. He was going to kill this thing once and for all! He'd had enough of its terror. With a reverse grip, he lifted the dagger above his head and leaped through the air like a scorpion poised to strike. But just a moment before he struck, the demon deftly stepped to the side, and Ethan stabbed empty air.

"Behind you, Ethan!" someone called, he wasn't sure who.

Heeding their advice, Ethan slashed blindly behind him, and felt the blade catch on something. Hopeful that he struck another blow to Inferius, Ethan turned around to see the demon was just a short distance out of his range, and there was a slash mark in the veins of the wall. *How is this thing so fast?*

It stood in front of him, not moving. Loosening his stance, Inferius opened his arms in the universal invitation to, *come and get me*. Ethan took the bait. He stepped forward on his left foot and used both arms to thrust into the creature's chest. The sound of the creature's skin cutting reminded him of the noise a wasp nest makes when cut. Then the blade continued into where the beast's internal organs should have been, but instead its insides had the consistency of mashed potatoes.

Somewhere behind him, Ethan heard one of his friends shout, "Ethan, what are you doing?" but he ignored it. Ignoring the shout wasn't too hard, everything around him sounded like his head was underwater. He turned back to the beast, beaming with a victorious smile. Surely it had to be dead now, right?

He was met with those horrible green orbs set in the thing's head. It pulled the dagger from its chest and threw it at the wall across the wide room. It stuck about ten feet in the air, just out of reach. Now it was the beast's turn to attack. It wrapped its horrible, spindly fingers around Ethan's neck. Of course, Ethan fought like hell, kicking and screaming and even biting, but it did nothing. All he got out of the experience was the taste of rotten meat.

It slammed him into the ground so that he was lying flat on his back, pinning his shoulders like they were in a wrestling match. Ethan squeezed his eyes shut and could feel the beast's gaze burning into him, but he knew that there wasn't anything he could do to fight it. He laid in wait for some assistance from his friends.

After what felt like ten minutes of laying under the beast's gaze, his friends had still not come to help, so he risked a peek to see what was going on.

He opened his eyes.

Immediately Ethan grew weak. It felt like his soul was being drained, and he could barely move at all. And this wasn't just because the creature had him pinned; his muscles refused to respond.

Remembering why he opened his eyes at all, Ethan searched the room for his friends and saw that they were struggling with something on the ground. The uneven floor blocked his view of their feet, so he couldn't tell what was going on, but they wouldn't be helping him anytime soon.

Then Ethan saw a red tendril reaching around Eric's calf. Eric kicked like a bull. The floor was holding them down!

Ethan slammed his eyes shut, and felt his strength return right away. Help wasn't coming, and he was pinned. He did his best to remain calm, but panic was setting in, and Ethan's breaths gradually became more rapid and shallow.

Something dripped on his forehead. Inferius wasn't restraining his arms, so he reached up to investigate. The fluid smelled of metal. It was slippery too, like… motor oil.

It's bleeding.

A few more drops fell from the wound in the creature's chest, and something shifted in Ethan's consciousness. A flicker of hope. An idea. All of it made sense. The staircase in the woods reacted violently to physical attacks, just like Inferius the demon, but instead of fighting fire, it nullified the fuel before it could even ignite. Fire scared it. Then Ethan came to find out that the blood running through this horrible place closely resembled motor oil. Ethan grinned despite the green gaze boring into him. "I've found your weakness," he whispered.

Reaching into his pocket, Ethan retrieved the book of matches that he originally brought to attack the stairs. He lit one and held it in one hand, then used his other to feel around the Inferius' chest. When he found its wound, he brought the match to the opening.

Inferius screamed.

This wasn't a scream of anger like before, this was one of pure, agonizing pain. It wasn't a steady roar, it fluctuated in pitch, volume, and sometimes it paused all together, as if the beast had to take a breath to continue the cry.

The grip around Ethan's neck and shoulders relaxed, too, then detached entirely. Ethan scrambled on his hands and knees to get away from the beast, and it did the same, crawling away from Ethan. Still on the ground, Ethan propped himself up on his elbows and looked at the demon.

It writhed on the ground with its lanky appendages seizing up and spasming. It looked like a dying spider. As the fire within its body spread, the skin of its back began to glow, and Ethan saw a misshapen ribcage backlit by the flames eating at the demon's insides.

Ethan watched the beautiful sight for a moment, then went to help his friends. Hurting the creature weakened the veins, but their grip was still firm on the men's legs. Ethan climbed the wall where the creature threw the dagger and retrieved it from its high perch. Once his friends were free, they stood to watch Inferius burn.

"You did it, Ethan!" Alex yelled in excitement.

"Don't sound too surprised," Ethan joked.

Williams' stared in awe. "All these years, and I never thought that its weakness would be fire."

The beast coughed and an orb of flaming oil flew from its mouth. It landed in a puddle of the black blood. The puddle burst into flames.

"We need to leave. Right now," Ethan commanded.

"But the entrance is still blocked," Mason said, "And we need to finish the job. Make sure its fully dead."

"Mason, this whole place is about to become Deepwater Horizon, and I don't want to stick around for that. There's no way this thing is going to survive. And I don't think we'll have any problem cutting through the barrier anymore."

With the dagger, Ethan went to the blocked staircase and sliced through the veiny mass blocking their way. Sure enough, it squirted and writhed at the assault, but did not grow back like before. One by one, his friends filed into the staircase, and he was the last in line.

Before leaving, Ethan turned to look one last time. Nearly the entire room was engulfed in flame, and the beast still hadn't given up. It was seizing and squirming on the ground, close to death, but not quite there.

It's out of my control now, Ethan reassured himself, *at least I know its weakness now.*

He ducked through the opening and rushed up the stairs.

Chapter 14

The moon was out. And so were the stars. At the sight of the night sky, tears welled in Ethan's eyes. He wasn't one to be emotional, but while he was down there, he internalized the realization that he would probably never see the sky again.

But there it was.

He stepped out of the cave's opening and was greeted with the tranquil sounds of nighttime. Crickets chirped somewhere in the distance, and Ethan thought he heard a bat flapping overhead. It must have been investigating the strange humans that emerged from a cave.

Ethan collapsed into a patch of grass, spreading out like a starfish. He felt a swarm of confusing emotions within himself, but he decided that he could deal with them tomorrow. Only one mattered to him now: pride.

There was an unspoken consensus among the group—everyone laid down like Ethan—that they would sleep the night here, and deal with everything in the morning.

Chapter 15

Ethan and Williams sat together watching the sunrise. "When do you think you'll be ready to start working with me?" Williams asked.

Gazing out at the conflagration in the sky, Ethan considered the question. He absolutely wanted to work with Williams. After going through the struggles of fighting the stairs, he discovered that he felt a great duty to his community. But he was still high on victory and didn't want to make any promises right away. "I don't know, I need some time to go home and decompress. I have plenty of savings to last for a few months without work, but I doubt I'll wait that long."

"I hope not, but you don't need to worry about money. I'm ready to put you on the Forest Service payroll. You have time to relax, you've done a lot, but we also have a lot of work to do."

Ethan breathed in the fresh, cool morning air, at peace with himself. "Alright."

| | |

The whole group hiked out together in the morning. Not much was said, there was nothing to say. Everyone was still in shock, but overall, they were happy with their accomplishment. Especially Ethan, who blamed himself for the near loss of Eric. They hiked beside each other.

When they reached the trucks, Williams caught Mason eyeing the bullet holes in his vehicle. "Sorry about that, Mason," he said while rubbing his neck, "I'll buy you a new truck."

Ethan frowned a little, "what about my truck?"

"Oh, I forgot to tell you in all of the action," Williams said, "don't worry about your truck and your gear. Surprisingly, it was undamaged in that spin maneuver you did. I have it stored in a Forest Service lot, safe and sound. I'll drive you, Alex, and Eric there."

"Okay," Ethan said, still a little mad about his truck being taken. "Well," he said, turning to Mason, "it seems that we'll be working together a lot more from now on, thanks for all the help. What you did to turn the tide for Alex and I was brave.”

Mason smiled a sad smile. “I’d be happy to stay in touch, but I doubt we’ll be working together all that much.”

“Why?” Ethan asked.

“I already talked to Williams about it, I’m transferring to the National Parks Service. Hopefully, it will be a lot less exciting, and I can help the community without dealing with,” he gestured in the direction of the cave, “all that.”

Ethan smiled, “I’m glad you’re making the right choice for yourself; I’ll be sure to stay in touch.” He pulled Mason into a tight embrace. “Until next time.”

With Alex and Eric, Ethan climbed into Williams truck. It still smelled new. They whipped down the road with the windows down.

Ethan wasn’t in the mood to talk, so he stared out the window, letting the wind flow through his hair. In the golden morning light, the forest looked happier. Based on the way Williams talked about all the work there was to be done, Ethan knew that darkness still lurked, but without Inferius lording over the forest, balance was restored.

Chapter 16

Two weeks passed. Ethan and Alex spent all that time at home, playing videogames, resting, reading, and sleeping in their own beds. Ethan was much calmer, and he was beginning to think that enough time had passed that he was ready to give Williams a call.

But when his cellphone rang, showing Williams on the caller ID, that decision was made for him. He picked it up. "John, is something wrong? I thought you wouldn't need me for a while."

Williams got right to the point, "when we were down there, I took some field notes from a dead man. Do you remember?"

Ethan nodded, then remembered that Williams couldn't see that over the phone. "Vaguely," he said.

"I used the information on that notepad to do some research, and I uncovered records of multiple secret expeditions down there."

"Okay, that was pretty obvious based on all the bodies, what's your point?"

"Inferius has been killed before. It's only a matter of time before he returns."

About the Author

Gavin Baird is the author of *The Genesis of a Ranger* and *Forbidden Climb*. He currently lives in Oregon, where he is at work on his next novel.

For more information, visit:

AuthorGavinBaird.com

Instagram: GavinBairdOfficial